"No one has seen her for hours?"

Trey looked at the sky with a rancher's eye. The storm, as bad as it was, looked like it was just getting started. "You're sure she didn't leave for a hotel in town? Maybe hitch a ride with some other guest?"

"This is hers." Emily held up a lady's purse. Even Trey knew a woman wouldn't leave without her purse. Emily handed him a Massachusetts driver's license. "Here's what she looks like."

Her signature was precise and legible. *Rebecca Cargill*. A pretty woman. Brown hair, with thick, straight bangs. As Trey took a moment to let the image settle into his brain, something about the expression on her face resonated with him. There was strain beneath that smile, a brave smile for the camera. *I know how you felt, darlin'. I was afraid I wouldn't pass the damned exam, either.*

* * *

Texas Rescue:

Rescuing hear

A TEXAS RESCUE CHRISTMAS

BY
CARO CARSON

MILLS & BOON

Published in Great Britain 2014
by Mills & Boon, an imprint of Harlequin (UK) Limited,
Eton House, 18-24 Paradise Road, Richmond, Surrey, TW9 1SR

© 2014 Caro Carson

ISBN: 978-0-263-91341-5

23-1214

Harlequin (UK) Limited's policy is to use papers that are natural, renewable and recyclable products and made from wood grown in sustainable forests. The logging and manufacturing processes conform to the legal environmental regulations of the country of origin.

Printed and bound in Spain
by CPI, Barcelona

Despite a no-nonsense background as a West Point graduate and US Army officer, **Caro Carson** has always treasured the happily-ever-after of a good romance novel. After reading romances no matter where in the world the army sent her, Caro began a career in the pharmaceutical industry. Little did she know the years she spent discussing science with physicians would provide excellent story material for her new career as a romance author. Now Caro is delighted to be living her own happily-ever-after with her husband and two children in the great state of Florida, a location which has saved the coaster-loving theme-park fanatic a fortune on plane tickets.

For William Edward,
A brave and brilliant boy

Chapter One

James Waterson III left his family's ranch at the glorious age of eighteen, ready to exceed the already high expectations of his friends and family, teachers and coaches. James the third, better known as Trey among the ranch hands and football fans, the recruiters and reporters, was going to conquer college football as the star of Oklahoma Tech University. He'd so easily conquered high school football, the NFL was already aware of his name.

At the age of twenty, Trey was washed up.

What's wrong with that boy? He blew his big chance.

What's wrong with him? He was so bright when I had him in class.

What's wrong with the Waterson kid? He must've gotten into drugs.

What a waste, what a shame, why, why, why?

His parents, of course, had left the family ranch in Texas to visit him in Oklahoma numerous times. They'd consulted with his coaches and met with his professors, and no one could understand why Trey Waterson, the promising freshman recruit, could no longer remember the play calls and passing routes now that he was a sophomore.

Well, Mr. Waterson, I'm not saying your son can't handle stress, but we've seen kids freeze up when they get in a big stadium. We're talking about a crowd of one hundred thousand.

No one could deny that Trey's test grades were no longer easy As, but struggling Ds and failing Fs.

To be honest, Mrs. Waterson, he was supposed to come to my office for tutoring directly after class, but he never showed. As I told the athletic director, I can't help a kid who refuses to be helped.

Trey's parents had believed him. He wasn't trying to skip class. He was not experimenting with drugs. They remembered the hit he'd taken in the last quarter of a home game, and worried that he was somehow suffering, months later.

We take good care of our players. Your son had a CT scan and passed a neurological exam that very week. Everything looks completely normal. No damage from that game, and no brain tumors or anything else that would explain the changes in his behavior.

That had been the most disheartening news of all. Trey was healthy, according to the doctors. An MRI was ordered, anyway; Trey was told it was "unremarkable." He could balance on each foot. He could touch his nose with his index finger and stick out his tongue straight and name the current President of the United States.

When he finally found his professor's office and correctly described how to calculate the area within the shape created by rotating a parabola around the z-axis, Trey believed the doctors, too. There was nothing wrong with him. He was just having a hard time, somehow. Not sleeping well, for some reason.

After their conversation, the professor gave him the exam, letting him make up the missed test just because Trey was the future of the Oklahoma Tech football program.

Trey failed the math test.

He understood the mathematical theory, but he couldn't calculate three times six. Five plus twelve. He sat in the professor's office and sweated clean through his shirt. He thought he was going to vomit from the fear, the sheer terror, of not being certain if he was counting on his fingers correctly. Seventeen times four? Not enough fingers, he knew that much.

We're sorry, Mr. and Mrs. Waterson. I know your son passed the drug screen, but these boys get pretty clever about hiding substances in urine samples. Now, now, hold up. We're not accusing him of taking drugs, but he has been cut from the football team. He has until May to bring his grade point average up to the school standard.

Trey came home for spring break, in time to help with the annual calf branding. As coordinated as ever, he threw lassoes and branded calves, day after day. He felt so damned normal, he wondered why he'd fallen apart. After spring break, he'd go back. He'd make up all the work he'd missed. He'd survive his nineteenth year. Then he picked up the branding iron, held it over the calf's hide and forgot which way was up. He was on the James Hill Ranch. The brand was a straightforward three initials: JHR. The iron didn't look right.

Trey had spun the brand the other way, but it looked just as wrong as it had at first glance.

Hurry up, the iron's cooling.

He must be holding the iron correctly, then, if they were telling him to hurry. James Waterson III permanently branded a calf on his own family's ranch with the symbol upside down.

He returned to Oklahoma Tech, failed all his courses, turned twenty years old and never returned home again.

It was much easier to lie to his parents on the phone. He had a good apartment, a good job, a good life. No, he wasn't going to go back to school next year, but that was okay, because he'd rather work with his hands. That became his big excuse: he'd rather work with his hands. His parents didn't need to know that he was spreading mulch for a landscaping firm.

His mother was worried sick, but he could fool her once a year when his parents came to visit. Before their arrival, he would practice driving from his one-bedroom apartment to their hotel and back, daily, until he could do it without getting lost. He'd preplan the restaurants they'd go to, and rehearse those routes, too. He'd smile and drop names as if he had lots of friends, and then his parents would leave after four or five days, and Trey would go back to his life of isolation and safe routine.

But now, he had to go back to the James Hill Ranch. Trey looked at the wedding invitation in his hand, at its classic ivory vellum and deep black engraving. It contained little squares of tissue paper and extra envelopes, a confusing piece of correspondence until he'd laid all the parts out on his kitchen counter.

Miss Patricia Ann Cargill
and
Mr. Luke Edward Waterson
request the honor of your presence
at their marriage.

The groom was his younger brother. His one and only brother. The wedding would be held on the ranch, one third of which Trey owned as his birthright. There was no acceptable excuse to miss his brother's wedding.

Ready or not, after ten years away from home, Trey Waterson had to return to the James Hill Ranch.

It was enough to make a grown man break out in a cold sweat.

Becky Cargill perched in her first-class seat, ice water in her hand, and sweated unladylike buckets. She'd never been so nervous in her life. Then again, she'd never tried to run away from home before.

The flight attendants were extra solicitous, even by the standards of the first-class cabin, but Becky didn't know if that meant she looked as ill as she felt, or if they'd simply seen her name on the passenger manifest. *Becky* meant nothing, but her last name, Cargill…well, that meant money. Of course, not everyone named Cargill was a relative of the Texas Cargill oil barons, just as not every Rockefeller or DuPont was one of *those* Rockefellers or DuPonts, but Becky's mother had indeed been married to one of *those* Cargills, and she made sure no one ever forgot.

Becky's birth father was not a Cargill, but when the man known to one and all as Daddy Cargill had been her stepfather, when he'd been in the first weeks of passionate fascination with Becky's mother, he'd let his new stepdaughter use his last name. Her mother wouldn't let her drop it now. Not ever.

Becky was her mother's little trophy, always dressed like a doll, the picture of sweetness and innocence. Her mother would turn on the charm for the Right Kind of People. *I'm Charlene Maynard*—or Lexington, whichever of her subsequent husbands' names was most in vogue, and then she'd gesture toward Becky—*and this, of course, is my sweet little girl, Becky Cargill.* By having a different last name from her mother, Becky was a useful sort of calling card, proof her mother had been accepted into more than one dynasty as a wife for the Right Kind of Man.

It was only recently that Becky had started to see that she'd been part of the reason men proposed to her mother. Mr. Lexington, for example, had enjoyed being photographed as the doting stepfather of a Cargill. In society page photos, it implied an alliance between the Lexingtons and the Cargills existed. For the Maynards, the appeal had been slightly different. That family had several young sons. Wouldn't Becky Cargill someday grow into just the Right Kind of Girl for one of their many boys?

Until she did, Becky was to be seen but not heard. She was to smile and not cry. She was to be pure and virginal and obedient at all times. Becky fingered the pearl button that kept her Peter Pan collar demurely fastened at her throat. Her style had not changed much since her mother had divorced Daddy Cargill. Becky had been nine years old at the time.

Now, she was twenty-four.

No one ever guessed her age. Her mother made certain of that, too. Becky had been shocked this summer when her mother had started dropping delicate hints to the Right Kind of Men that although Becky was indeed young, she was approaching a certain *desirable* age.

Shock had turned to devastation this winter weekend when her mother had, rather viciously, told her it was time for her to show her appreciation for the lifestyle which she'd been privileged to enjoy. Hector Ferrique, old enough to be Becky's grandfather, was the owner of the Cape Cod vacation home in which they'd been living this year. Apparently, it was time to thank Hector for the free use of his spare mansion, and for the first time in her pure and virginal life, Becky was expected to do the thanking.

Hector will arrive this evening, and we're all flying to the Caribbean to spend the Christmas holiday. I've packed your things.

The flight attendants noticed when Becky fished in the seat pocket for the air-sickness bag. "Can I get you anything else? Perhaps a ginger ale or some crackers?"

Why don't you line up about five of those little bottles of scotch on my tray table?

But, no. She'd never had five shots of any kind of alcohol. She was on her own for the first time, and she was going to need all her wits about her. Besides, she'd probably get carded, as usual, and that would be the straw that broke the camel's back. She might possibly cry. Or get angry.

"The ice water is just fine, thank you. Can you tell me why the plane hasn't left the gate yet?"

"They are waiting on the weather forecast for Austin. They won't let us take off if the destination airport is going to close due to ice and snow."

Becky looked out the window at the snow-covered Boston airport. "It snows every day."

"Yes, but it's unusual in Texas." The flight attendant tapped her wristwatch in a cheerful, apologetic manner. "They'll update the airport status on the hour, and then we'll know if we're cleared for take-off. Don't worry, Miss Cargill, we've got agents standing by to help you make alternate transportation arrangements if the flight is cancelled. You'll have first priority, of course. We'll get you home for the holidays."

Of course, since her last name was Cargill, the flight attendant had assumed Texas was home. Becky simply smiled, a display of pink lip-glossed sweetness, and the attendant moved on to the businessman in the next row, tapping her wristwatch, repeating her apology.

Becky dabbed at her upper lip with her napkin, mortified at the nervous sweat she couldn't control. She could feel a single bead of moisture rolling slowly down her chest, between her breasts, but, of course, she would not dab there.

Mother must have noticed my absence by now. She'll call the airport, and I'll be taken right off the plane, like a child. They won't card me first, not when she calls and says her daughter is on the plane without her permission.

Miraculously, the pilot came over the speakers and announced that they were going to take off. Becky's stomach went from fearful nausea to desperately hopeful butterflies. Within minutes, they began taxiing down the runway. She was leaving Boston, and her mother, and the horrible man to whom Becky was expected to sacrifice her virginity.

The pilot's voice was female, and somehow, that made Becky feel better. The only person Becky knew who could possibly defend her against Hector Ferrique was also a female, and a female pilot was going to get her there safely in an ice storm. With any luck at all, the snow and ice would arrive immediately after they landed, and it would become impossible for her mother to chase her down.

The plane lifted off. Becky had gotten away. Now, she needed to stay away. Even if the Austin airport closed after Becky arrived, her mother could and would find her and drag her back, unless Becky could find someone strong enough to stand up to her. There was only one person in her life who'd ever seemed stronger than Mother, and that was Daddy Cargill's real daughter, Patricia.

The year that Becky was nine, the year that her

mother had married Daddy Cargill, was the year that
Becky had worshipped her new stepsister, Patricia.
Eight years older than she, Patricia had swept home
from boarding school on weekends and vacations to
keep Becky's mother in check. Heavens, she'd kept
her own father in check. Becky had watched in wide-
eyed wonder as Patricia had plucked the key to the in-
nermost vault of the wine cellar right out of Mother's
hand. *I do think there are plenty of other vintages for
you to enjoy. Let's save the Cote de Nuits for an appropriate occasion, shall we?*

Then Patricia had given Becky a whole can of Dr
Pepper and let her drink it in her bedroom. Sitting at
Patricia's tri-fold vanity mirror, Becky had played with
real, red lipstick.

The divorce was inevitable between their parents,
of course, and one day, while Patricia was away at her
boarding school, Becky and her mother had moved out.
Becky had cried and said she wanted to be a Cargill.
Her mother had agreed that keeping the name would
be wise, which wasn't what Becky had meant at all.

This morning, as Becky's mother had announced
that Hector Ferrique would be coming to visit his own
beach house, the newspaper had announced that Patricia Cargill was getting married in Austin.

Becky had seized on those lines of newsprint, using
them as her excuse to get to the airport. How easy to
finally use that Cargill name, the one she'd been bor-
rowing since fourth grade, to change the chauffeur's
schedule. "No, my flight leaves this morning. Mother's
will be later this afternoon. My sister, Patricia Cargill,

is getting married in Austin this weekend. I'll be at the wedding while Mother and Hector are in Bimini. No, just the three blue bags are mine. The rest are Mother's. Thank you."

Becky was hoping the Cargill name would let her crash a wedding she hadn't been invited to. If her mother came to drag her away, Becky hoped the bride would kick her former stepmother out of the reception—but let her former stepsister stay. Indefinitely. As plans went, it was weak, but it was all a pure and virginal and obedient person like herself had been able to come up with on a moment's notice.

Please, Patricia, don't kick me out. I'm still just little Becky Cargill, and I've got nowhere else to go.

Chapter Two

Becky peered through the gray haze of winter weather at the endless county road. She spotted another gate for a ranch up ahead. Two posts and a crossbeam in the air, that was the standard ranch entrance in Texas. She'd already turned her rental car into two properties that weren't the James Hill Ranch. At the first, she'd gotten flustered and made the tiny car's engine produce horrid sounds as she put it in Reverse. After she'd driven through the second wrong gate, which had clearly been labeled the River Mack Ranch, making her feel like an idiot, she'd tried to make a U-turn to avoid the reverse gear. The U-turn had worked, but all her belongings had been thrown around as the car bounced over rough ground before making it back onto the road.

Becky could make out a letter J on the fence beside the upcoming gate. If the J stood for James, then she hadn't gotten lost after all, although the clunky GPS system, emblazoned with the rental car company's logo and bolted onto the car's dash, had gone silent many miles ago. She was officially out in the middle of nowhere on a two-lane road that had no name, only numerical digits the GPS voice had rattled off before losing its satellite connection.

Her phone, however, still had a signal. It rang again, shrill after being jarred out of the leather purse Becky had stuffed it in. Her mother was calling. She should answer.

Becky gripped the steering wheel. She couldn't answer the phone. She rarely drove anywhere, and she'd never driven this kind of car, so she had to concentrate. Snow had been falling, rare enough in December, apparently, to make it the sole topic of conversation in the Austin airport. The snow was beginning to look more wet, like sleet.

She would not panic. She'd just keep two hands on the wheel, and she would not answer the phone. *I'm twenty-four years old. I can drive a car in bad weather.*

She hadn't wanted to. At the airport, her request for a taxi to the James Hill Ranch had been met with so many chuckles and "you're not from around here, are you?" responses, she'd given up and gotten in line for the first rental car desk she saw.

Too late, she realized that her mother would be able to use the credit card transaction to find her. Becky had never seen a credit card bill, but she knew her mother could check it, somehow, almost immediately. She hadn't dared to use her credit card without permission since she was twenty-one. That year, her mother had placed her in a ski school in Aspen with teenagers who belonged to the Right Kind of Families. When her fellow students had learned Becky was actually of legal drinking age, they'd convinced her to buy the booze to go with their energy drinks. The next morning, her mother had asked her to produce the liter of vodka that she'd purchased in town at precisely 8:19 p.m. the evening before. Becky had been confined to her hotel room the rest of the trip—and she'd learned a valuable lesson about credit cards.

The phone rang once more. Her mother had probably tracked her credit card already. *Why did you rent such a low-budget car? Look at you, arriving at the Cargills in a rental car like a poor relation. You could have at least taken a limo, for God's sake.*

Becky hadn't gone to Daddy Cargill's mansion. She read more sections of the newspaper than her mother did. Outside of the society pages, there'd been a featured real estate listing for the infamous mansion. Photos of the outrageously tacky décor had accompanied the article. Patricia no longer lived there, and obviously had not for years.

Patricia was getting married at the James Hill Ranch. That was Becky's destination. Her best hope for sanctuary.

"Shoot!" Becky realized she was driving right past the gate. She hit the brakes and turned the wheel, but the snowfall had become ice, and the car spun wildly. Her seat belt held her in place, but her head thunked against the side window before the car came to a halt, facing the wrong way.

I will not cry.

The car's engine made that awful sound as she put it into Reverse.

I will not cry.

Everything in the car—up to and including her teeth—rattled as she traveled over a cattle guard on her way through a second, more elegant gate of wrough iron and limestone pillars.

I will not cry.

She presented herself at the door. She'd never before seen a housekeeper who answered a door while wearing jeans. She'd never been greeted by a staff member with "howdy" instead of "good morning, miss." Becky requested that Miss Cargill be notified that her sister, Miss Cargill, had arrived.

"Sure, uh-huh," said the older woman in jeans. "Come in, sweetheart. It's freezing out there."

Too late, Becky surmised that this was not a housekeeper. She'd probably just given orders to a relative of the groom. The woman did not introduce herself, however. She just launched right into a conversation as if they were acquainted.

"If you're here for the wedding, I've got some bad news. It's been cancelled. Didn't you get a message from your sister? I swear, she called a hundred people yesterday herself.

"The pastor was afraid to drive, and the caterers were in a tizzy. Luke and Patricia, they decided they didn't want to miss their honeymoon, what with the airports closing and all. They're taking some gigantic sailboat from Galveston all the way around Florida to the Bahamas. Anyway, they took their license to a justice of the peace first thing this morning and got married. Now Luke's parents are driving them all the way to the port to make their boat on time. But we're supposed to cut into their cake and send them a video of us doing it, so stick around, honey."

Patricia was gone.

Becky's cell phone rang, shrill.

"May I use your powder room?" Becky asked, smiling sweetly, although her pink lip gloss had faded away hours ago.

She locked herself in the bathroom, and she cried.

"Why, it's James Waterson the third, as I live and breathe! Aren't you a sight for sore eyes? I swear, you are even taller than your brother. What are you now? Six-three? Six-four?"

Trey steeled himself against the onslaught. He hadn't had a chance to scrutinize the woman's face, yet she was hugging him and patting him on the cheek, treating him like he was a growing boy when he'd just passed his thirty-first birthday. Clearly, she knew him, but he did not know her. If she'd just hold still and let him look at her face for a moment—but she chatted away, turned and dragged him from the door.

He hadn't had a chance to look about as he'd come in. He preferred to pause and get his bearings when he entered a new building, but this stranger gave him no chance. Trey looked around, consciously choosing to focus on what his eyes could see and deliberately ignoring the sounds hitting his ear. He was tired from the strain of travel, and he could only take in so much.

The woman pulled him into the high-raftered great room, and Trey, still concentrating on visual information, immediately focused on the fireplace. It was decorated for a wedding with a swag of fluffy white material and silver Texas stars, but he knew what it would look like without all that. He knew that fireplace.

Massive, its limestone edifice rose from floor to ceiling in a severe rectangle that would have been boring if the limestone variations hadn't been unique from stone to stone. Trey had lain before roaring fires, staring up at the limestone, idly noting which were white and beige and yellow, which were solid, which were veined. From infancy, he'd done so, he supposed. He last remembered doing it with a girl while in high school, drinking his mother's hot chocolate before sneaking his sweetheart out to the barn for some un-chaperoned time.

Yes, he knew that fireplace.

Suddenly, the whole room fell into place. Hell, the whole house made sense. Trey knew where he was. It was effortless. The kitchen was through there. The mudroom beyond that. His bedroom was down the hall. The dogs needed to be fed outside that door, every morning, before school.

There was nothing confusing about it.

God, he knew where he was. Not just how to navigate from here to there. Not just enough to keep from looking like a fool. He really and truly knew where in the world he was.

"Can you believe they ran off like that? I mean, you can't blame them with the storm coming and every-thing, but..." The woman squeezed his arm conspirato-rially. "Okay, I blame them a little. I think most women would want the wedding. You could always take a trip some other time. I mean, it's the bride's big show with the white gown, being the center of attention, the flowers, the cake, you know? But Patricia, she's some kind of sailboat nut. I don't even know what you call those people. Instead of horse crazy, are they boat crazy? Anyhow, you would have thought your brother had never wanted anything more in his entire life than to get on a sailboat and go visitin' islands."

With a woman? Someone he loved enough to pledge his life to? Trey didn't find that so hard to understand. It sounded as if Luke had made the choice between wearing a tux for one day or spending a month on tropical seas with the woman he wanted the most. His little brother had never been stupid.

Then again, once upon a time, Trey hadn't been stupid, either. Now, he didn't recognize the person he was talking to. He tried to place the woman's face as she chattered on.

"Luke's always been a cattle rancher, not a sailor. I guess people do crazy things when they're in love. I hope it lasts. Lord knows, none of my marriages have. I don't blame you for not coming to any of them."

Trey had been invited to her weddings? That sick, sweaty feeling started between his shoulder blades.

The sound of the mudroom door slamming centered him once more. It was a sound Trey hadn't heard in ten years, yet it sounded utterly familiar, instantly recognizable without any effort.

The man's voice that followed was new to him. "No luck, sugar," it boomed.

"Oh, dear. Trey, come meet your new uncle."

Uncle. That meant this woman was his aunt. Trey looked at her, and suddenly it was so incredibly obvious. She was his mother's sister, his aunt June. How could he have forgotten that he had an aunt June?

He felt stupid.

The kitchen, however, he remembered. He hadn't stepped fully into the room, hadn't put both boots on the black-and-white-checkered floor, when he felt that utterly certain feeling once more. His brain worked for once. He didn't just recognize the kitchen, he knew every inch. This drawer held the silverware, that cupboard held the big pots, and the cold cereal was on the bottom shelf of the pantry. He knew all that without trying, and it made him realize how little he usually knew about other rooms. He'd been adrift in every room he'd been in for the past ten years.

His new uncle shook hands, then shook his head at Aunt June. "No sign of her, sugar."

Another woman, younger than Aunt June, came in from outside. He could see her through the doorway to the mudroom, stamping her boots and smacking icy droplets off her jacket sleeves. "It's turning into sleet out there, bad."

He didn't know her.

She knew him. "Ohmigod, Trey! I haven't seen you in ages." She dumped her coat on the mudroom floor and came rushing at him, arms open. They closed about him in a hug, unfamiliar in every way.

Don't panic. Think. Aunt June has daughters. Think of their names.

Aunt June patted his arm and started laughing. "I don't think he recognizes you, Emily. It's been ten years, at least. You were in pigtails and braces last time he saw you."

He had a cousin named Emily, of course.

Stupid, stupid, stupid.

Just to prove that he knew *something*, he opened the correct cabinet to pull out coffee mugs. His brother hadn't moved their mother's traditional coffee machine. It sat on the same counter it had always sat on. Trey knew the filters would be in the cupboard above it.

"Can I make y'all some coffee?" he said, his voice sounding gruff to his own ears. He owned a third of the house, and he had company. He ought to make some attempt to be a host.

"That's a good idea," Emily said. "I need to warm up before I keep looking."

And…he was lost again. The emotions of these three people were hard for him to keep track of. Everyone was happy one moment, worried the next.

"What are you looking for?" he asked, determined to make sense of the world. He started counting scoops of coffee into the filter basket. *One, two, three, four—*

"This girl named Becky disappeared."

Six, seven—crap. He'd lost count. Trey decided the amount of coffee looked about right, shoved it into place and hit the power button.

"You gonna put some water in there, sugar?" Aunt June asked, laughing.

Damn it.

But everyone was happy again for a moment, chuckling about old age and forgetfulness.

Then, they weren't happy. As Trey filled the carafe with water, his aunt started explaining who was missing. A young lady had arrived for the wedding, Patricia's sister, or so she'd said. They hadn't known Patricia had a sister.

"Just as sweet as can be," his aunt said.

"Pretty as a picture," his uncle said.

"She seemed nervous to me," Emily said. "Then she stood in a corner, and I saw her listening to something on her cell phone. She just put on her coat and mittens and hat, and walked out the door. I thought she was going to her car to get something, but she never came back."

Aunt June looked out the picture window above the kitchen sink, angling her head so she could cast worried looks at the sky. "It's been hours."

The coffeepot was brewing perfectly, making soothing noises. The scent of fresh coffee filled the kitchen. Trey knew where he was. He knew who everyone was around him. He ought to be content, but apparently, the part of him who'd been born a cowboy wasn't dead. Someone on the ranch was unaccounted for, and that meant trouble.

"No one has seen her for hours?" he asked, and he looked at the sky with a rancher's eye. The storm, as bad as it was, looked like it was just getting started. "You're sure she didn't leave for a hotel in town? Maybe hitch a ride with some other guest?"

"This is hers." Emily held up a lady's purse. Even

Trey knew a woman wouldn't leave without her purse. Emily handed him a Massachusetts driver's license. "Here's what she looks like."

Her signature was neat and legible. *Rebecca Cargill*. A pretty woman. Brown hair, with thick, straight bangs. As Trey took a moment to let the image settle into his brain, something about the expression on her face resonated with him. There was strain beneath that smile, a brave smile for the camera. *I know how you feel, darlin'. I was afraid I wouldn't pass the damned exam, either.*

She could have been stressed over any number of things, of course. It was fanciful of him to imagine he knew what the look on her face meant.

"I'm sure she's found shelter by now," Aunt Jane said.

Trey looked up from the driver's license in his hand. "If she hasn't, she'll die tonight. It's too cold to survive without shelter."

Aunt Jane made a horrified little sound, and Trey cursed himself. He hadn't always been so blunt. Hell, people had called him charming in high school and college. Now he had to work not to blurt out every thought that passed through his thick head.

His new uncle put a protective arm around his wife. "She's probably fallen asleep in the hayloft in the barn, and she just hasn't heard us calling for her. She'll be fine."

Emily darted a look at her mother, then pressed a cell phone into Trey's hand. "Here's her phone. It's not password protected. I didn't want to be nosy, but I thought there'd be more photos of her."

Trey started sliding his thumb over the screen, skimming through the photos stored on the phone. They weren't very personal. Seascapes of some rocky shoreline that looked nothing like the Texas coast. Distant children wading in the surf, silhouetted against a sunrise. A couple walking away from the camera, holding hands.

Finally, he saw a more typical snapshot of a woman holding a mutt. Trey was able to mentally compare this woman with the one in the driver's license. Not Rebecca Cargill.

He slid his thumb across the screen once more. The next shot was also of the mutt, but this time, it was held by the woman on the driver's license. Same pretty face. Same brown bangs. Same strain beneath the smile.

"She looks so young," his aunt said, looking over his shoulder. "I can't believe her license says she's twenty-four, can you?"

Emily was looking over his other shoulder. "I thought we could use that photo if we needed to call the sheriff."

That snapped Trey into action. He handed Emily the phone as he addressed his aunt and uncle. "You haven't called the sheriff? Dark's coming. There isn't much time to get a search party out here."

"Your foreman, Gus, he's got the ranch hands doing the searching. They've been stomping all over the grounds. She couldn't have gone that far on foot."

His foreman? Trey didn't have a foreman. Luke did.

Trey hadn't set foot on the ranch in a decade. With his parents traveling ten months out of the year as retirees, Luke was the Waterson who ran the James Hill Ranch. Luke had decided to promote their longtime ranch hand, Gus, to foreman. Trey had only agreed over the phone. He supposed it was just by virtue of being a Waterson that Aunt June addressed him as if he were still part of the James Hill.

Trey turned to Emily. "The sheriff's got helicopters. We don't. Call them."

She ran to the house phone, the one that still hung on the kitchen wall as it had for the past twenty years or more.

His aunt patted his arm. "Honey, even the big Austin airport has been closed for hours now. They aren't puttin' anything up in the sky while ice is coming down out of it."

"That may be true, but we'll let the sheriff's office make that decision. I'm not a pilot. I'm just—"

He stopped himself, then turned on his heel and headed back to the front door, past his father's arm chair, past his mother's lamp, the one he and his brother had broken and glued back together. He picked up his sheepskin coat where he'd left it and shrugged it on.

Aunt Jane followed him. "You're just what?"

He chose a Stetson from the few hanging on pegs by the door. Whether his father's or his brother's, it didn't matter. The men in the family were all built the same. It would fit.

"I'm the only Waterson around here right now, and

I'll be damned if a young woman is going to die on this ranch on my brother's wedding day."

He crammed the hat on his head, and headed out the door.

Chapter Three

I am not going to die today.

Becky forced herself to stop sliding down the tree trunk.

Stand up, Becky. Straight. At least pretend you've got some confidence, for God's sake.

The landscape of central Texas all looked the same. As far as she could see, stretches of scraggly brown grasses were broken up by scraggly waist-high bushes. The only color she saw was her own pastel-pink ski parka, chosen by her mother for appearance, not survival.

Who am I going to impress with this fake Cargill confidence, Mama? But she stayed on her feet.

She spotted an occasional cactus, which proved that Hollywood didn't lie when it put a cactus in a cowboy movie. But there was no shelter. As she'd driven the ATV four-wheeler away from the barn, ice had crunched under her wheels. Although the exposed skin of her face had been stung by the wind almost immediately, she'd kept driving, feeling like the control she had over the loud engine was the last bit of control she had in the world.

She'd turned up her collar and buried her chin in her jacket, and kept going. Somewhere. Away from the house that her mother would find. Far from the house and the barn and the sheds, she'd crossed acres of ground that shined in the afternoon sun, for they were completely covered in a thick but beautifully reflective sheet of ice. By the time the next bank of storm clouds had rolled in, hiding the sun and killing the enchantment of her ice world, she'd been low on gas.

She'd turned around—a U-turn that was easy in the right kind of ranch vehicle—and started heading back, but she hadn't made it far before the engine had run out of fuel.

That had been hours ago. Literally, hours ago. Forced to seek shelter as the wind picked up and fresh sleet started to fall, she'd left the bright blue ATV out in plain sight—as if she'd had a choice—and she'd headed for a line of trees. Gnarled oaks had seemed not too far away, and clusters of shockingly green cedar trees were interspersed among them. They weren't much, but they were more shelter than the ATV provided.

They weren't close, either. She'd begun sweating as she crunched her way across the uneven land, so she'd unzipped her coat to let any moisture evaporate. One thing she'd learned while skiing in Aspen was that getting wet when it was freezing outside led to intolerable cold. Even the most devil-may-care snowboarders would have to get off the mountain and change into dry clothes when they worked up a sweat.

The Aspen ski school had included some lessons on building emergency shelters. Too bad Becky didn't have ski poles and skis with her, because they'd been used to build every kind. Too bad there was no snow. In Aspen, the snow had been so deep, they'd dug a trench that they could sit in to escape from the wind.

Actually, the instructors had dug the trench. The rich kids and Becky had just sat in it. Some survival training. Maybe she would have learned more if her mother hadn't tracked her credit card so closely.

I'm going to die because some teenagers convinced me to buy them vodka. I missed the rest of the survival lessons because of vodka. And Mother.

She wouldn't cry. The tears would freeze on her cheeks.

She huddled against the trunk of the largest oak. It provided a little protection from the wind, at least, but the bare branches blocked nothing from above. Ice was falling from the sky, and it was falling on her.

She was so cold. She could just slide down this tree, take a little nap…and never wake up.

Stand up. Straight. For God's sake, Becky, your shoes can't hurt that badly. You will stay in this receiving line and shake hands with the club president before I give you permission to leave.

Becky stomped her boots to stay awake. With each thump of the ground, she heard the thud and she felt the jarring impact, but she realized, in an almost emotionless acknowledgment of fact, that she could no longer feel her feet.

I could possibly die today.

It would be so unfair if she died. Damsels in distress were supposed to be rewarded for trying to avoid a fate worse than death.

Well, she'd avoided going to the Bahamas with Hector Ferrique, all right, but she couldn't say if that fate really would have been worse than this one. For starters, although it sounded repulsive, she didn't know how difficult it was to have sex with a man one didn't like. She didn't know how difficult it was to have sex at all.

I'm going to die a frozen, twenty-four-year-old virgin. Out here, no one will find my body for months. Maybe years.

Terror made her colder. She would not give in to terror.

She needed to find some way to cover her head, because the snow or rain or sleet or whatever it was had started soaking through her ski hat. Its high-tech material was water-resistant, but apparently not waterproof. It could only repel the sleet for so many hours.

Becky looked around for smaller, broken branches on the ground and gathered them up, clomping her way from one to the other on her numb feet like a frozen Frankenstein. Her arms were growing numb, too, so she stuffed the twigs and thin branches haphazardly into a fork in the tree's lowest branch.

The bare sticks weren't going to block many drops of icy rain. Becky looked at the green cypress trees. She remembered them from her elementary school days. They were tall and narrow, green from ground to the top, and when she was a little girl, she'd been very aware that adults complained about them incessantly. She stumbled her way toward one now, thinking its evergreen branches would be useful stacked on top of her bare sticks.

The cypress tree disagreed. Becky got as good a grip as she could manage, but the flat, fan-like greenery slipped through her gloves like it was coated with wax or oil. Frustration made her eyes sting with more tears she couldn't shed. The exertion of tugging and pulling was making her too warm in her coat, yet her feet weren't warming up at all with the activity.

She tried a new approach, stomping on the lowest branches with her clumsy Frankenstein feet. She lost her balance several times and grabbed at the slick greenery to stay upright, but she succeeded in breaking a few branches off at the trunk.

In triumph, she carried them back to her twig roof and layered them on top. Then she hunkered underneath her little roof, hugged the oak tree's trunk to keep the wind from whirling around her, and she waited.

For what?

There was nothing to wait for. Help was not coming. No one knew her at that ranch house. Her mother had left her a message about how she'd tracked her to the Austin airport, but it would take her time to get here and more time to figure out that Becky had gone to the groom's ranch, not the Cargill mansion. It was getting dark already. Mother would not find her tonight.

I left the ATV out where anyone could see it overhead.

There was nothing flying overhead, however. No planes. No helicopters. Nothing would come searching for her by air, not while this storm raged. It could be another day or more before anyone at this ranch realized an ATV was even missing. When the storm was over, when they could search for her, it would be too late.

Sweet little Becky Cargill, the good and obedient child, had defied everyone's expectations and run away.

Now sweet little Becky was going to die.

Trey could find Rebecca Cargill. Of that, he had no doubt. The only question was, would he find her before she succumbed to the cold?

Hang in there, miss. I'll be there soon.

All he needed to do was guess where *there* was.

Had she left the house on foot, Gus and the ranch hands would have found her by now. Trey checked the barn as a formality, but he knew she hadn't taken a horse. The cowboys would have noticed one was missing, and the horse itself would have had the sense to buck her off and run back to the warmth of the barn.

That left the ATVs. Trey walked out the other side of the barn, turned up his collar against the biting cold and crossed the yard in long, rapid strides to the outbuilding where they'd always kept two ATVs. Sure enough, one was missing.

She'd left the spare two-gallon gas can on the floor. The sight of that gas can sitting on the concrete slab, forgotten, chilled Trey in a way the weather could not. If the gasoline was here, then she'd run out of gas *there*. The only way she'd make it back to the ranch was if he went and got her.

He'd known that, too, standing in the black-and-white kitchen.

He shut the shed door against the howl of the storm and started tying supplies onto the back of the second ATV. It only took him minutes, thanks to the miracle of having his memories of the ranch. He'd gone camping with his brother, when his brother had wanted to learn how to build a campfire. Gone fishing with his father, when his biggest problem had been deciding if he liked baseball or football better. Gone riding the fence line after his last football game as a high school senior, checking all seventy-five thousand acres of the main section of the ranch with the foreman. He knew how to survive outdoors on the James Hill Ranch.

Trey rolled the ATV out of the shed, shut the door as Miss Rebecca Cargill had, sat on the ATV as she had and started the engine. Tracks led in every direction from the shed, and with the ground hard with ice, none of them look fresher than any other. Instead, he looked to the horizon and tried to view the ranch through her eyes, so he could guess which way she'd decided to go.

The strained girl in the driver's license photo had needed to get away. She'd shown up to a wedding where no one knew she existed, and a phone call had sent her right back out the door. He couldn't imagine what from, but she'd run. He didn't know why, but she'd wanted to be alone. Badly. Immediately.

Straight. She wouldn't have headed to any of the scenic spots like a visitor would, nor had she gone to check the water level in the creek like a ranch hand. She'd only needed to get away from some kind of situation that had no other solution, so she'd left her phone and her purse and her life, pointed the ATV away from the house and gone.

She'd driven as fast as she could, eating up the gas. She'd wanted space. Freedom. So as Trey drove, he chose the most obvious routes and the most level ground, keeping the last signs of civilization at his back. At every decision point, he chose the easiest path, the one that would allow him to get as far away as quickly as he could. And when his gas tank was on empty, he saw the bright blue ATV parked in the middle of one of the most remote pastures on his land.

He'd found Rebecca Cargill, because he'd known that she'd been running from a fate she couldn't control. He understood that emotion.

The year that he'd turned nineteen, he had done the same.

Chapter Four

The storm was getting worse. Becky's time was getting shorter, her body getting colder, her lungs struggling as the air temperature dropped lower and lower. She wanted to sleep, oh, so very badly. Staying conscious in the constant, inescapable cold had worn her out in a way she'd never experienced. If only she could sink down among the oak's roots and sleep…

She would die. When she finally closed her eyes today, they would not open again.

She wasn't ready for that.

There was so much she hadn't experienced. Her entire life, she'd been waiting to start living. Wrapped in her demure cashmere sweaters, standing still by her mother's side, she'd been waiting for permission.

Waiting to meet a wonderful man. Waiting to have her own home, a permanent home, the kind that children would return to every Christmas, even when they were grown with families of their own. Waiting to live a life Becky knew existed for other people, one full of ups and downs, one she wanted to experience for herself.

Now, she was waiting for a miracle.

She curled her arms around herself a little tighter and slid down the tree trunk. She looked up at the little roof that had kept the worst of the sleet off her head and shoulders. She was afraid her meager attempt at shelter had only delayed the inevitable. Really afraid.

She couldn't stay on her feet any longer, but she kept her eyes open, because she did not want to die yet. One little miracle, that was all she needed.

"Rebecca Cargill!"

She shuddered in misery as she imagined an angry male voice shouting her name. When the brain froze, did one suffer delusions before dying?

"Rebecca!"

Goodness, that sounded so real.

"Where are you, darlin'?"

It was a miracle. Somewhere close by, an angry man was her miracle.

Here, I'm here, she tried to call. Her jaw had been so tightly clenched against the cold, she couldn't force the muscles to relax so she could speak.

I'm here, I'm here, don't leave me. Please, don't leave.

She hugged the tree trunk instead of herself. Using her arms as much as her legs, she hauled herself back to her feet.

"Rebecca. Good God."

Before she could turn around, she was swept off her feet, wrenched away from her tree and held against a man's chest instead. She wanted to throw her arms around his neck, not because it felt like he might drop her, but because she was so grateful he was here. But her whole body was so stiff, her arms wouldn't obey her brain.

"Stay with me, darlin'. We'll get you warmed up. Just stay with me."

Did he think she'd rather stay with that tree? That tree had not cared that she was there. Now that she was not alone, she realized how very lonely she'd been. Hour after hour, she'd been the only living creature. Even the birds and insects had disappeared into their own shelters. It had been Becky and a tree. And ice.

His boots crunched over the ground as he carried her, and he seemed to take very long strides and move very quickly. It was disorienting, to suddenly be with another human being. She was no longer alone. Thank God, she was not alone.

"Okay, Rebecca? Are you with me?"

I'm trying to answer you. Give me a minute. Her jaw didn't want to unclench, but she nodded.

He looked down at her then, and over the scarf that covered the lower half of his face, under the brim of his cowboy hat, she tried to make eye contact, but he wore wide ski goggles.

Goggles. The concept burst into her brain like they were a new invention. How convenient goggles would have been while riding in the cold wind. Every inch of his face was covered, which made him seem incredibly smart to her. And beautiful. The mere fact that he was here made him the most beautiful person on earth.

"Was that a nod," he asked, "or just a shiver?"

She tried to smile at her beautiful rescuer, and she thought she'd succeeded in making her frozen facial muscles move, but he only looked away again, and kept walking.

He can't see my face, either.

She hadn't been smart enough to prepare for this weather, so she'd had to make do. She'd pulled her ski hat down low and her collar up high, but her eyes had been exposed, so a few hours ago, she'd taken the long strings of her ski cap and wrapped them across her eyes and tied them behind her head. She could see out through the slit in between them.

They'd reached an ATV, a black one, and the man set her on the seat. "Let me get you a blanket— Hey!"

She had no balance. She'd tried to grab for the handlebar, but her disobedient body hadn't responded and she'd started to do a face plant into the ground. The man had reflexes like some kind of ninja, because he caught her. Keeping one hand on her, he tugged at some gear behind the seat and produced a blanket. It looked like a giant sheet of aluminum foil, but Becky knew it was a thermal blanket.

Despite the term "thermal," it didn't look warm, and when the man sat behind her on the ATV and started tucking it around her shoulders, it didn't feel warm, either. He positioned her in his lap, moving her so that she sat sideways. He pulled her arms, one by one, over his shoulders, and she tried to hold on to his neck as she pressed her face into his icy coat.

He started the engine. "Just a few more minutes. Stay with me a little longer, Rebecca."

I'm not going anywhere, she tried to say. It sounded more like, "Nnn…ing…anywhere," but her rescuer chuckled and she felt the wonderful rise and fall of his chest through his coat. He tucked the top of her head under his chin and started the engine.

At the first bump, she found her arms were too weak to hold on, but he kept her from falling. With one arm wrapped tightly around her, he steered the vehicle one-handed. The metallic blanket kept some of the wind off her, but she was not warm, and it would take hours of this driving to get back to the ranch house. She wouldn't last.

She couldn't fight the cold any longer, but at least she would not die alone. A strange sort of content-ment filled her.

I got my miracle. I was found.

Rebecca closed her eyes. Secure in her rescuer's arms, she drifted into black oblivion.

Trey felt the woman's arms slip, limp, from his neck.

He kept driving, keeping a sharp eye out for the landmarks that had not changed. There was an old cabin a half-mile away, built near the banks of a creek. It had been abandoned for the past hundred years, ex-cept for the ranch hands who'd found it better shel-ter than none when caught in a sudden rain, and the rancher's sons who'd found it to be a handy hide-out. The creek had not moved, of course, so Trey felt ab-solutely certain of where he was, where everything was around him.

Thank God. If there was ever a time he couldn't af-ford to get lost, now was it.

"Rebecca. Keep breathing." He gave her a little shake. "Breathe, damn it. That's all you gotta do, honey. Breathe."

The cabin was situated within a trio of the largest mesquite trees Trey had come across in either Texas or Oklahoma. Someone had added a corrugated metal roof decades ago, for which Trey was grateful. It probably wouldn't leak. The fireplace was stone, and it looked to be standing fairly straight after all these years. Trey parked the ATV under a mesquite, knowing it would still become coated in ice, but the need to care for equipment as well as one could had been ingrained in him since birth.

He held Rebecca in his arms and stepped warily onto the narrow porch. Nearly half the boards were missing, but the ones that remained held his weight as he lifted the simple wooden crossbeam and opened the door. Setting Rebecca on the floor on top of the silver blanket was like laying down a rag doll. Hypothermia could be deadly and quick. He had no time. He ran back to the ATV, grabbed everything with both arms and ran back into the cabin.

He shouted her name and ordered her to breathe as he unpacked the single sleeping bag and laid it on top of a second metallic thermal blanket. Then he started to strip. Basic survival rules required skin-to-skin contact to stay warm. There was no time to gather wood and build a fire. Traveling farther was out of the question.

He shed layers, starting at the bottom. His boots, her boots. Socks. Pants. Any cloth in direct contact with skin held moisture, so their underwear had to go, too. Modesty meant nothing when death was threatening.

The air was freezing in the cabin, but he didn't dare slip her into the sleeping bag until every last stitch of clothing was off. If he slid her legs into the bag while her coat was still on, the coat could drip water onto the bag, and then they'd never get warm in a damp cocoon.

"C'mon, Rebecca. Wake up. Help me out."

She responded to his voice by stirring on the silver blanket, but that looked like it was all he was going to get from her. Still, it was something. She wasn't deeply unconscious. Maybe she was just exhausted, if he was lucky.

He took off the last of his clothing and went to work on hers. Damn it all to hell, it was cold, and he started to shiver, although he'd taken off her hat, gloves and coat in seconds. He would've had a hard time getting all the tiny pearl buttons of her sweater undone in any circumstances—it was a garment guaranteed to make a man think a girl was off-limits—but with the shivering and the cold and the seconds ticking by, he quit on the second button and ripped the shirt down the front.

It took two shaking hands to undo her bra clasp and toss the damp elastic to the side. Immediately, in a move that was more about speed than gentleness, he rolled her into the sleeping bag, yanked the zipper closed from her feet to her waist, then jumped in beside her and yanked the zipper shut the rest of the way. The one-man bag was designed to cover the head and left only a circle for the face. Although there were two of them sharing the circle, he pulled the opening's drawstring, making that circle even smaller, keeping just that extra bit of cold out.

He'd just zipped his naked self in with an ice cube. He'd once had a girlfriend whose feet were always so cold, she slept in wool socks. This woman was cold like that all over. It scared him, honestly, to feel skin so cold over an entire body.

"Time to warm up," he said, and he started moving his hands over that icy skin, trying to stimulate her circulation without damaging any skin that might have gotten frostbite.

She didn't move. He kept at it. She would warm up, because he wouldn't let her do otherwise. This was the most effective method possible. The cabin protected them from the worst of the weather, although the chinks in between the log walls were plentiful. They shared a sleeping bag that was undoubtedly rated for far colder conditions than this. They would survive, even without a fire.

And without their clothes. Trey hated himself for thinking about such a thing in the circumstances, but as he pulled Rebecca tightly against himself, he was quite aware that she was a woman. He'd heard a soldier in Oklahoma complain over a glass of beer about survival training with men. His instructor had required everyone to go through the hypothermia drill, the entire hypothermia drill, to force the men to overcome their aversion to sharing body heat like this.

Trey tucked Rebecca's legs between his. She was an ice cube, but she was a smooth and feminine ice cube. Frankly, if he had to share some "full frontal" with a stranger, he couldn't deny that a young woman was a highly preferable hypothermia partner. Still, they'd

probably be embarrassed as hell about this someday—
which was better than being dead.

"Come on, wake up and share this awkward moment
with me. Rebecca, wake up and talk to me."

They were on their sides, facing each other, nearly
nose to nose. As he stroked up her back to the nape of
her neck, he drew his head away a little bit to take a
look at her face, now that it wasn't hidden under hat
and strings and collar.

His hand stopped. She was almost unnaturally beautiful. Her face was heart-shaped, framed by bangs.
Her brows and long lashes were a rich brown. But the
hypothermia made her skin appear to be white porcelain, and her lips were blue with cold. The effect was
startling, like holding a life-sized version of the porcelain angel that his mother put on their Christmas tree.

Acting on instinct, Trey pressed his mouth to hers,
keeping his eyes open, staying for a long moment to
allow the heat of his mouth to warm hers. He didn't
want this beautiful woman to have blue lips.

When he felt her lips softening under his, he lifted
his head and brushed her hair behind her ear. Her lips
looked a little less blue in her perfect, heart-shaped
face. He wondered what color her eyes were.

"Come on, sleeping beauty. It's time to wake up. Let
me see if your eyes are as beautiful as the rest of you."

Trey closed his eyes when he kissed her this time,
as though it were a real kiss.

Rebecca woke up.

Chapter Five

When Becky had closed her eyes, she hadn't expected to ever open them again, yet here she was, awake. She was alive, but she was still cold. Shivering, and sick of it.

The first millisecond of opening her eyes was spent on realizing she was alive. The second millisecond was much more interesting. She was looking right at the jaw of a man, a real man with a five-o'clock shadow and a firm mouth. But as she stared at that mouth, the man kissed her.

Her eyes fluttered shut once more. His lips were soft, but the greatest miracle of all was that they were warm. Oh, so warm—and she craved heat right now.

She loved that mouth, so she kissed it tenderly, then opened to taste his upper lip, his lower. If his lips were warm, than his tongue was warmer, and she lost herself in a good, hot French kiss.

He pulled away, and she opened her eyes once more to focus on his mouth as he spoke.

"Okay, then. I'd say you're awake."

She looked into eyes as blue as the summer sky.

But she was still cold, and it felt as though she would

never stop shivering again. His warm hand stroked down her back, stilling her momentarily as it passed, and then she shivered again.

Her breasts brushed against the warm skin of his chest. His warm skin was just that. Just skin. Nothing else. Awareness came swiftly. Her breasts were bare. Startled, she made a sudden movement, her legs sliding against his, smooth against rough. She was bare everywhere.

"Oh, dear. We're—we're—"

"Kind of awkward, isn't it? But we won't freeze to death."

She looked away from his blue eyes to focus on her surroundings. They were hiding in some kind of cocoon, but she could see through the opening. Somehow, he'd magically surrounded them with a log cabin while she'd been sleeping.

"Where are we?"

Gosh, that was such a cowardly question for her to ask. She should have addressed the fact that they were utterly naked, but she went with the log cabin. She was like Mother, after all, ignoring the difficult and unpleasant issues, even if they were more important. When her mother had heard that her latest paramour was already married, she'd pointed to a purse and asked about its designer. Becky was nude and so was this man, but she was asking about location.

"We're in the old Tate cabin. It was built more than a century ago. Lucky for us, they built them to last back then."

She could see outside through some of the spaces

between the logs. She could *feel* outside, gusts of damp cold. She burrowed into the sleeping bag, which meant she tucked herself more tightly against his naked body.

"The wind can come right through this cabin," she said against the warmth of his throat.

"Some of it does. We'd be worse off if we didn't have these walls. That storm is getting bad outside."

Well, that was blunt. "How are we going to get back to the ranch?"

"You mean the house? We're not. We're going to stay right here, and stay warm."

"And naked?" There, she'd addressed the elephant in the room. She wasn't a total coward.

"It's the best way for us to stay warm."

Becky cared about being warm more than anything else. "I'm so tired of shivering. It hurts."

"I imagine it would. Hadn't thought about it before. Having your muscles clench like that would wear you out. Don't worry, you'll stop shivering. You're no longer unconscious, so that's an improvement. I'm glad you're awake."

His large hands roamed all over her body, as she realized they'd been doing this entire time.

"Are you really glad I'm awake?" she muttered. "Because it seems while I was asleep, you got me naked."

"Strictly survival, Miss Cargill. When I undress a woman for fun, I like her to be awake and fully participating."

Undressing for fun. She knew people got naked to have sex, of course, but she'd never considered that the actual taking off of clothes was one of the fun parts. He made it sound worth trying.

"And kissing me? That was strictly survival, too?"

"Your lips were blue."

The way his gaze dropped to her lips when he said it made her stop shivering for a second. He was a darned good-looking man, in that outdoorsy, cowboy kind of way. And he'd found her. He was her miracle.

"What's your name?" she asked, watching him as he watched her lips.

"Trey Waterson."

"Tell me, Trey, are my lips still blue?" It was the single most provocative thing she'd ever said in her life, and she'd said it to a naked man. She bit her lip, wishing the words back.

He drew his palm up her spine and over her shoulder, to rest on her neck. With his thumb, he caressed her jaw as he frowned at her mouth, taking her question seriously.

"They're more pink, but still too pale."

He bent his head, and kissed her again, softly, slowly, and without the openmouthed hunger she'd had. It was a lovely kiss, all the same, and she felt rewarded for having been daring.

Then he rested his head next to hers, so they simply looked at one another in the last of the winter twilight. They could have been friends sharing the same pillow, settling in for a long slumber-party chat. The corners of his mouth curved upward in a bit of a smile. "You're going to make it, you know."

She was still shivering, but at his words, she realized the waves of shivers were coming and going, their intensity diminishing with each return. Her jaw wasn't clenched to prevent her teeth from chattering. Her arm was wrapped around his warm body instead of clinging to the bark of a tree.

"Thank you." How terribly inadequate that sounded. "I mean, thank you for my life. Not 'thank you' like you just passed the mashed potatoes. There ought to be a better word to say. Thank you so much, because I really didn't want to die."

"I know you didn't."

"It was practically suicidal, the way I left. I can see that now, but I wasn't trying to kill myself, honest."

"You were just running away. People don't think real hard when they do that."

She shivered, and pressed her entire body closer to him for shelter. For protection. She hid her face between his warm neck and the sleeping bag.

His hand swept down her back, firmly over her backside, too, to the back of her thigh. He lifted her thigh just a tiny bit, adjusted the position of her leg. "Can you feel your feet? Your toes?"

She flexed her ankle and tried to wiggle her toes. They didn't exactly respond with individual wiggles, but she felt them pressing into his calf muscle. "They're still there. I'll never take my feet for granted again. You should have seen me out there, clomping around like I had cement boots. It's so hard to walk when you can't feel your feet."

"I wouldn't have let you stay out there long enough to clomp anywhere."

She almost smiled at that, remembering how he'd scooped her off her feet before she'd seen him coming. Her shivers subsided, and she moved to be able to see his face once more. Night had come, but their eyes had been adjusting all along, and moonlight poured through the cracks along with the cold air.

"Thank you," she repeated.

His soothing hand had just traveled over her shoulder. He stopped and squeezed her upper arm. "You don't have to keep saying that."

"I need to. I'm so grateful, you can't imagine."

With a sigh, he turned a bit so he was laying more on his back. "All right, then. Get it out of your system."

He looked like he was waiting patiently for something. "Thank you?" she said tentatively.

He nodded, solemn. "You're welcome, Rebecca."

She stared at him in the moonlight.

After a minute, he raised an eyebrow. "Is that it? Are we done?"

She gasped, a tiny sound of indignation. "Are you joking about this?"

He started to laugh.

She gave his shoulder a little shove. "If it weren't for you, I would have died."

"I'm glad you didn't." As if that was the end of it, he started maneuvering around in the bag. "I'm going to unzip this for a second—"

"No! I'm not warm enough."

"Just far enough to get my hand out. You need to drink this water before it freezes solid. Your body is working hard to warm up. It needs water." He grabbed for a canteen that was in a pile of other stuff, jostling them both. She felt her breasts bounce a little against his arm. She was embarrassed, but he didn't seem to notice as he brought the canteen back inside and zipped the bag.

"I think we'll have to sit up so you can drink," he said. "Ready? One, two, three."

Of course, they had to move at the same time. One person couldn't sit up in the sleeping bag if the other was laying down. She tried, but curling up into a sitting position was more than her body was ready to do yet.

"It's okay. Let's try that again." Trey put his arm underneath her and lifted her with him as he sat up.

"Thank you," she said.

"I knew there were more thank-yous in there. Drink up."

She felt those blue eyes on her as she chugged, suddenly realizing how terribly thirsty she was. When she finished, he wasn't looking at her any longer. Instead, he was frowning at the night sky beyond the cracks in the log wall.

"The wind has stopped, but the clouds have cleared up," he said. "We're in for a cold one."

"It looks nicer than this afternoon."

He made a negative movement of his head and hand. She felt every bit of it, sitting so close to him. "Cloud cover keeps some of the earth's heat in. Today's clouds dumped their sleet and left, so now there's nothing to stop the temperatures from falling." He took the canteen from her and unzipped the bag, efficiently setting it outside again.

"Falling? It's going to get colder than it already is?" She could feel the fear crawling up her throat.

He looked at her with concern. After a long second, he kissed her forehead. "Listen to me. Outside, the temperature may fall, but you are not going to get colder. You and I are going to stay right here, safe and sound and warm."

He laid her back gently, following her down and settling her body against his again. *Safe and sound and warm.* As a seduction, no man could have had her more completely in his thrall. There was something about him that made her feel restless inside, reckless. They were alive, the only two people in the world, and she couldn't get enough of his deep voice and his soothing hands.

She set her hand on the back of his neck and tilted her face to his. She wanted to be *kissed and held and warm.* She let her eyes drift shut, anticipating the feel of his mouth.

"It's not us I'm worried about," he said. "It's the cattle."

"Oh." She blinked, feeling a little sheepish. Cows had never crossed her mind, but apparently, even if virginal little Becky Cargill was naked, a man's thoughts didn't stay on her. Hopefully, he hadn't noticed that she'd been about to kiss him. "What—um, what do cows do when it's this cold?"

"The foreman knew this weather was coming. He probably got a good portion into the calving sheds. The rest would've been driven into one of the pastures that has a deep gully. The cattle huddle in there to get out of the wind and basically do what we're doing."

"Nice to know I don't have the common sense of a cow. I drove into a wide-open space. I was so stupid. It would have served me right if—"

His finger pressed her lips, cutting her off. "Don't say that. Ever. Do you hear me?"

She was so surprised at his ferocity, she couldn't even nod. She just stared at him, his face a shadow in the night.

"You got yourself out of the wind as much as possible. You built yourself a shelter. You stayed alive. Give yourself some credit, Rebecca. You've got common sense and you must have a giant heap of willpower, because you were still alive when I found you. Thank you for staying alive until I could get there."

He moved his finger away from her lips only to cup her head in his hand. He angled her so he could kiss her, not so softly this time.

"Thank you," he said against her mouth, "for staying alive. This works both ways. You didn't want to die, and I didn't want to find you dead. I feel this insane relief that you are with me. You did a phenomenal job of staying alive. Thank you."

He was kissing her again almost before he was done speaking, and this time, she felt the sweep of his tongue. They were tasting, kissing, and she wanted to absorb all the intensity of him, all that heat, into her body. For the first time, she realized he wanted to feel her heat, too, finally greedy as she was.

I feel this insane relief that you are here with me.

That was it, exactly. To hear him say what she was feeling was like another miracle.

He ended the kiss first, still cupping the back of her head in his hand, now panting slightly over her lips. "Rebecca, I—"

She waited, but words seemed to fail him, and he rolled a little bit away, onto his back. He exhaled, a sound that she feared sounded like he was disgusted with himself. Perhaps he thought she was too fragile for kissing? Perhaps he didn't know that she shared his feelings.

Perhaps she ought to be brave enough to stop waiting for her life to begin. If she wanted to kiss this man, perhaps she ought to tell him.

"You're welcome," she said quietly.

"What?"

"You said 'thank you,' so I'm saying 'you're welcome.' I want you to know that if kissing is your particular way of saying thanks, then I hope you have a whole lot of it to get out of your system. You are one great kisser."

The night was utterly, completely silent in the remote cabin. She heard her own heart beating, too loud because she'd been too bold.

He started to chuckle. Then he gave her a tight, friendly squeeze, and let her go. He planted a kiss on top of her head, like they were pals.

Swell.

"I've got to step out for a minute." He started unzipping the bag.

He was leaving her. Alarm made her turn abruptly

and push up onto her elbow as he slipped out. "You can't go. You'll freeze to death."

He'd pulled a Navajo-style blanket out of the gear and thrown it around his shoulders like a cape before she could catch more than a glimpse of his nude, male backside in a stripe of moonlight.

He stomped on one boot. "I'm not going to relieve myself in front of you, darlin'. I'll be back in a minute. Stay warm."

He stomped on the second boot, and left.

Rebecca flopped back down, and shivered. So much for her first attempt to grab life by the horns. She'd told a man he was welcome to kiss her, and he'd left to go find a tree.

I will not cry.

That never would have happened to her mother. Rebecca had never wanted to be like her mother, until tonight. In this one thing, she now wished she were. She wished she had the power to make Trey Waterson crazy about her.

Rebecca, he'd called her, and she hadn't corrected him. Rebecca sounded like a woman who was confident. A woman whom men would want to kiss. She was still sweet Becky Cargill, and she felt like she always would be.

Very quietly, and only for one minute, Becky turned her face into the material of the sleeping bag, and gave herself permission to cry.

Chapter Six

You are one great kisser.

She'd said that, looking at him with those doe eyes in that heart-shaped face, porcelain perfection brought to life. Rebecca had told him he was a great kisser, and Trey had very nearly blurted out every thought that passed through his stupid brain. *You're beautiful. We're alive. Let's have sex.*

Thank God, he'd controlled it. He was grateful for every trial he'd failed in the past ten years, because those situations had taught him the hard way to relearn how to think before he spoke. He knew he was often too blunt despite his best efforts, but at least tonight, when faced with the greatest challenge of all, he hadn't made an idiot of himself in front of Rebecca Cargill.

You are one great kisser.

I want to do a hell of a lot more than kiss you.

That would have scared her. She would have been on guard and anxious no matter how hard he tried to explain that he didn't mean those outbursts. It didn't mean they weren't true—it meant that he did know better than to say such things. He just seemed to know it after the words had come out.

When he'd first been kicked out of Oklahoma Tech, sex had been the one, sweet oblivion where he didn't have to *think*. He didn't need to monitor himself. *That lingerie looks sexy as hell. Come here, so I can take it off you.* The unfiltered truths that came out in bed seemed to make women happier, and for that, he was grateful.

But the girlfriends had been fewer and farther between over the years. It was difficult to date a woman when you couldn't reliably find her house, and he was tired of the strain. Relationships that did last a little while had to end before anyone got too serious about moving in, settling down, having children. Trey had cared about each girlfriend, enough that he wouldn't have saddled any one of them with a husband that couldn't count the change at the grocery store.

A relationship with Rebecca Cargill was out of the question. She was something special. It would be impossible to keep things purely physical with a woman whose emotions were so vulnerable, but whose personality was turning more playful with each passing moment.

She'd impressed him just by surviving. She'd impressed him again with how well she'd taken it in stride when she'd woken up, stark naked, with a man she didn't know. He'd tried to set a casual tone about the situation, and he was doing his best to keep his private parts private, shifting out of the way so she wouldn't be pressed against parts of a stranger's body that she wouldn't want to know so intimately.

She was recovering quickly, and the more she re-

vived, the harder it got. There were times she seemed
almost innocently unaware of the position of their bodies. Didn't she realize that she was sometimes cuddling
into a position that would have allowed him to enter
her easily, if they'd been making love?

No, at least twice now it hadn't seemed to occur to
her, so he'd been the one who'd moved, who'd shifted,
who'd tried to keep things polite, naked as they were
in a sleeping bag.

Keep things polite. That's all he had to do. He had
to lie down with a beautiful woman who thought he
was a good kisser, and not touch her nude body while
they kept each other warm by touching.

Hell. He didn't think a man with a good brain could
make sense out of that one.

He had no choice. It was a waste of time to freeze
out here, when there was no way to avoid another round
of innocent, sensual torture with Rebecca. It was time
for this landscaper to cowboy up.

He lifted the crossbar and went back to her dangerous warmth.

Rebecca's one-minute crying jag did not go unpun-
ished. They never did. She should have known better
than to think that without Mother around, it was safe
to cry.

Her tears had ended with a shiver, right between the
shoulder blades. Too late, she realized she should have
been zipping up the bag when she'd been indulging in
her tears. Trey hadn't left her uncovered, of course,
but even the slit left by the open zipper let in too much

cold for her system to handle. She zipped the bag with fingers that shook. She huddled, her arms crossed over her chest as they had been all afternoon.

The first time her teeth clacked together with one of those convulsive reactions to being cold, she panicked.

"Trey!" she cried into the darkness.

The door had opened the same moment as her teeth had chattered, but she'd called his name, cold and fear making her desperate, although he was coming back to her already.

He dropped to his knee beside her, Navajo blanket spreading over them both. "What happened? Talk to me." He started running his hands over the sleeping bag. "You're shivering again."

"Come back, p-please."

He was already hauling off his boots. He fumbled for the zipper a moment, then climbed in beside her.

His skin was not as warm as it had been before, not after his time outside. Rebecca squeezed herself to him, anyway, hanging on for dear life.

His hands began their familiar journey, over her shoulder, down her spine, over her backside and to her thigh. The motion was steady, unrushed, when she was frantic to get warm. He used his voice like he used his hands, speaking calmly and evenly.

"I'm sorry, baby. You're going to be okay. It won't take long this time. Those shivers are going away."

The mantra repeated as his hand smoothed its way back up her body. "I'm sorry, baby. You're going to be okay, it won't take long."

"What took you so long?" she said against his shoulder.

"I was only gone a few minutes."

"It was an eternity."

"I'm sorry. I didn't realize you were that vulnerable. You're dehydrated, and you need food, so I guess your body is just not going to be able to handle much cold for a while, not until we get you watered and fed."

"Watered and fed like a good little cow." She had to laugh at his cowboy talk.

"That's right." She could hear the smile in his voice as he kept stroking her, soothing her, caressing her.

Petting her. *He's probably petting me like I'm a horse.* Even that thought made her smile. He was a cowboy, so she couldn't expect anything less. She didn't want anything less. This felt perfect.

"We'll warm up for a while, then we're going to eat and you're going to drink more water, okay?"

"I wish the warming part went faster. I swear, I want to sink my teeth into your shoulder. You know, to keep them from chattering."

"Yeah, well… God." He cleared his throat. "We'll talk to keep your teeth from chattering. Where do you live?"

"Boston, this season. Cape Cod. I'm a city slicker. Isn't that what you cowboys call us?"

His hand stopped. Changed course. "I'm not a cowboy."

She felt, instinctively, that was not true. "How do you know this ranch so well?"

"I was raised here, but I live in Oklahoma now. I've got a landscaping business, nothing large."

Feeling warmer, she cuddled into him, sliding her knee up the outside of his thigh. His hand stopped her knee when it reached the top of his thigh. He smoothed his way down her calf and ankle, then held the arch of her foot in his warm hand for a moment. It felt nice, but it kept her from positioning her knee in a more comfortable way.

"What do you do for a living?" he asked, his voice low and deliciously husky.

"My mother likes me to accompany her to her engagements."

He was quiet. She imagined a cowboy or a landscaper wouldn't know what to say to that.

The tip of her nose was cold, so she nuzzled it into the dip above his collarbone. "I don't have a real job. It would be nice, but my mother thinks it would make her look bad. She respects old money, the kind where someone's ancestors earned it a few generations back. She likes people who don't have to work."

"But you think it would be nice to have a job? Most people would think that not working was nice, if they could get away with it."

"It's a lot of work, to keep an income flowing so that you don't need to work."

Her mother was always on alert, always aware of who was hot on the social scene. Clothes and hair and body were in a constant state of updating for Mother. For Becky, they never changed. The right events had to be attended, so that invitations would be extended to others. Events were where Mother met men, men with old money. It was a full-time job, and Becky was her best accessory.

"Do you mean investments?" Trey asked. "Interest?"

"Something like that." Rebecca thought of Hector Ferrique, lending them one of his vacation homes. He wouldn't have lived in it this winter, anyway, but nothing was free.

"So, how are you related to the groom?" she asked, changing the subject just like Mother had taught her. "You have the same last name."

"Brother. You're the bride's sister?"

"Same last name, but no. Stepsister. Not even that. Our parents divorced fifteen years ago." She kept it light. Matter-of-fact.

"It's nice that you two are still close. That makes you a better sister than I am a brother."

Take the compliment, Becky. When someone has a good impression of you, for God's sake, don't correct them.

Mother was right. Mother was always right. Except, when Becky had been about to die, alone by a tree, she'd thought her life with Mother was all wrong, wrong, wrong.

She took a long, slow breath, in through the nose, out through the mouth. She breathed in cold Texas air and warm male skin. She breathed out...so much that she'd been holding inside.

"I'm not a good sister at all."

His hand squeezed her instep. "I'm sure that's not true."

"I crashed the wedding. I hadn't seen Patricia in years, not until Mother had the chance to take a little trip a few months ago and needed somewhere for me to go. She dropped me off at the Cargill place."

"You needed a babysitter?"

"We were between houses. She was kind of between men. She's kind of a professional wife."

"That's a lot of 'kind of.'"

"She's been married four times, to really wealthy men. Five, if you count my father."

"You don't count Daddy Cargill? How rich are the other men when an oil baron doesn't make the top four?"

"I'm Patricia's stepsister, remember?"

He was silent a moment. "Yeah, you told me that, Rebecca."

"It's Becky. Just Becky. I'm not even a Cargill. My father is some lazy son of a bitch bastard who didn't know his right from his left."

"Your mother's words?"

"Correct. It is the only time swearing is acceptable."

"Your mother's rules?"

"Correct again. But she was married to him, so she's been married five times."

"Going on six?" He was holding her instep tightly.

"I don't think so. She's only forty-five years old, and she looks smashing, to be honest. But I think those men put her in the bedmate category now. They like to take her on vacations. She looks good, and she can be a great conversationalist over dinner, a good travel partner. But when it comes to marriage, those men expect someone who is child-bearing age. You've seen the gray-haired guys who marry a supermodel who has their baby. The guy can be sixty years old, with some pregnant wife his daughter's age. I think it proves their virility, and all that."

Trey didn't speak for the longest time. Becky realized she had stopped shivering and felt warm again, but she missed the soothing stroke of his hand, although the way he held her instep was very...nice. Strangely intimate, to have her feet warmed by a man.

She set her hand on the rounded shaped of his shoulder. He remained still, so she drew her hand down his arm. It had to be twice as big as her arm, fascinating in all its hills and valleys. She followed it all the way to his hand, made a little U-turn on the back of his hand with her fingertips, and started sliding back up again. Stroking him was as soothing as being stroked by him.

"That is the life you know?" he said, with that husky note back in his voice. "Old men who expect young women to marry them for their money?"

"And prove their virility by walking around with a pregnant belly in the latest designer's maternity wear. Don't forget that part."

"But you left, and crashed a wedding."

Her hand rounded his shoulder. She could press hard into his muscle; there was so much of it. With a deeper touch, she traveled down his biceps. "Mother wanted to go on another vacation. Christmas in the Caribbean. Who wants to spend Christmas in the Bahamas?"

CARO CARSON 69

"Apparently, my brother and your sister do."

His dry humor surprised her. "One, she's really not my sister, remember? And two, it's their honeymoon. That's different. A regular Christmas should be cozy at home. I want a big Christmas tree with a family all around it, opening gifts and drinking hot chocolate, like you see on TV."

"You haven't had that, not even as a child?"

"Kind of. When my mother married into the Lexingtons, they put on the big family Christmas. I always kind of felt sorry for the staff, though. It was like we were supposed to enjoy a big Christmas, but they weren't. They made all our beds while we opened the presents. We ate the big meal while they stood in the dining room, wearing the black-and-white uniforms to serve the turkey and mashed potatoes. I tried to help clean up the wrapping paper one year, but that was a big no-no. My mother said they were paid time and a half on holidays, and not to do their jobs."

He kissed the top of her head. She was used to being treated like a child, but with him, she didn't like it.

"You don't have to feel sorry for me," she said. "I'm not a child anymore."

"I know. That kiss was for the little girl you used to be. You tell her I think she's a sweetheart for being sympathetic toward people who have to work on Christmas."

He made her heart hurt, saying that. She wanted to cry, but crying never turned out well. She lapsed into silence, determined to close off that little piece of her heart. She could think about it some other time.

He let the silence last a long while before he spoke. "You listened to a message on your cell phone before you took off. That's what my cousin said."

Becky only nodded in reply. It was easier to ignore that little ache in her heart if she concentrated on his body. She kept pressing her fingers into him, sliding down his forearm.

"Rebecca, why did you run away? What were you so afraid of?"

When she reached his hand, she slid her foot away, and interlocked her fingers with his. It was as if her hand wanted intimacy, but her voice stayed light, joking, impersonal, even though she spoke the truth. "It was simply awful. I handled it so badly."

She tried to laugh at herself, a society laugh like her mother would have used. *Oh, kids these days. They can be so crazy. What can you do about it except wait for them to outgrow those teen years?*

"I ran away because I didn't want to be forced to spend the week naked in bed with a stranger. Ironic, isn't it?"

She laughed as if she had a martini in her hand and diamonds around her throat, but Trey, he didn't laugh at all.

Chapter Seven

"So your mother is a—" Trey swallowed the only food he'd thrown into the survival gear. It was beef jerky, which took forever to chew, and which gave him a chance to search his lame mind for the right term. "Your mother is a call girl?"

"Oh, my goodness. Not at all. She would never consent to a one-night stand. Men court her. They woo her. They buy her diamonds and take her to the Riviera."

"Here, finish this water bottle. They take her to the Riviera without sleeping with her?" He knew he sounded as skeptical as he was.

"She always insists on separate rooms. It makes them all the more eager to take her on trips. They're hoping she'll consent to sleep with them, I'm sure. Until the past few years, though, she held out for marriage, every time. She's a big believer that men won't buy the cow if they get the milk for free. Now she holds out for the long-term affair. A house. Vacations. You've got to show her you mean to keep her around for a while."

As if Rebecca hadn't just told him about a way of life that violated everything he'd been raised with, she took a hearty bite out of the beef jerky. "This is the best beef jerky, ever, and I'm not just saying that because I'm starving."

Trey scrubbed his hand over his face. He was having a hard time being sure he'd heard what he thought he'd heard. She reported it all so factually, without seeming to be involved herself, yet she was telling him about her life. A real life. She really lived with a woman who'd made a career of marrying rich men.

"Where do you fit in the picture? You said your mother likes you to accompany her to what, exactly?"

The thought was there, of course, of sick bastards who would sleep with a mother and move on to the daughter. It happened. That it could happen to Rebecca made him feel ill. Angry. Willing to fight.

"It's taken me a long time to figure it out, but I'm her proof that she's fertile. Men want to prove their virility with the young wife, right? Well, as long as she has little Becky around, I make her look younger than she is."

"Little Becky? You're twenty-four."

She seemed startled by this, sitting up even straighter in his arms.

They were sitting up in the sleeping bag to eat and drink, but the bag wasn't wide enough for them to sit side by side, hip to hip, without stretching the fabric. Instead, Rebecca was a little in front of him. Trey had managed to jerk some of the sleeping bag's material up between his legs, covering his crotch a bit, so she could sit between his thighs without her backside pressing directly against— Well, that would have taken awkward to a whole new level.

"How'd you know I was twenty-four?"

He bit off another chunk of the beef jerky. It bore zero resemblance to the garbage one could purchase at an Oklahoma gas station, because it was made here on the ranch. He handed it back to her. "I saw your driver's license. Eat some more."

She obeyed, and knowing more of her life story, it almost bothered Trey that she was so compliant. She needed the food more than he did, however, so he couldn't complain that she was obediently eating it.

"My driver's license," she repeated, sounding disappointed. "No one ever guesses my age. For years now, I've been passing as eighteen. Mother encourages it."

"You don't have the body of a teenager."

She stopped chewing.

Trey cursed himself, and the stupid way he blurted things out without thinking.

"I don't?" she asked, and damn if she didn't sound hopeful.

He ran his hand down her thigh as he had a hundred times tonight. "Not that I'm trying to—but it's pretty obvious—yes, you're built like a woman." He scrubbed his face once more. "This is a hell of a conversation."

"If you'd seen me with my clothes on, you wouldn't think I was all grown up."

He remembered the cashmere and its little-girl collar. All those damned buttons. "By the way, I ruined your sweater."

She waved a hand dismissively. He couldn't see it, of

course, but he could feel the movement in the sleeping bag. "There's more where that came from. She dresses me very demurely."

"Why don't you buy your own clothes, then?"

"She tracks my credit card."

The final piece of the puzzle fell in place. *It would be nice to have a real job,* she'd said. She was ready to be free of her mother's life, but she had no way to do it on her own. He'd crashed at a teammate's house when he'd first left college. He'd slept on a friend's couch for a couple of months when he started working for a landscaper, so he could save up enough for that first-month and last-month rent on an apartment.

Rebecca's mother made sure she had no money of her own. When she'd been backed into a corner, Rebecca had run to a former stepsister for help. It hurt Trey to know that her closest relation, her only hope for an ally, was a former stepsister. Poor, isolated Rebecca.

"I'd assumed you were running away—"

"—from a fate worse than death," she finished for him.

It wasn't what he'd been about to say.

"When I was hugging that tree and waiting for a miracle, I had a lot of time to think. I realized that I've been too patient. All this time, I've been waiting for permission to leave."

They'd eaten all the food and drunk all the water they wanted. There was nothing left to do but sleep or talk. Rebecca leaned against him, like he was her support, and she seemed to settle in for a long chat.

Grateful for the material that kept his awareness

of her body from being too obvious, he listened. He caressed her, because it had become a habit. And he dropped an occasional kiss on her shoulder, because she was in his arms and she didn't object and her skin felt smooth beneath his lips.

"I read a newspaper article about the foster care system," she said, as though talking in the dark like this was something they routinely did. "It focused on foster kids who were aging out of the system. That was the term they used, aging out. I realized that was what I'd been doing with my life, waiting to age out. Eventually, I'd have to get too old for my mother to keep pretending I was eighteen. I thought she'd release me, and I'd finally get to go to college or get an apartment, or something exciting like that."

Caress. Kiss. Listen.

"But I found out at six this morning what aging out meant. She'd told Hector Ferrique that I was twenty-one. He likes his women young, she said, but he doesn't want to risk any messy legal troubles. To be told I was twenty-one when he'd assumed I was younger…it was a little Christmas present from her to him."

Rebecca crossed her arms over her chest in that self-preserving way she had. He crossed his arms over hers, and held her tightly.

No one will hurt you while I'm around. But he didn't say it out loud.

"We were to fly out at four this afternoon. His home in Bimini had a marvelous location, she assured me, but only two bedrooms. It would be best if I stayed in the master suite with Hector. Mr. Ferrique. I should continue addressing him as Mr. Ferrique, unless he asked me to do otherwise. It makes me seem younger, you see. I'm already on the pill, of course. She's had me take that for years, just in case. I'm not to bother Hector about any other precautions."

Trey knew every inch of her skin, every shiver of every muscle. He knew exactly when her first tears fell. He kissed her shoulder, and kept her wrapped tightly in his arms, and swore to himself that Hector Ferrique would never touch her.

"At four this afternoon, I was nearly dead. You think sleeping with a man in Bimini is the worst thing in the world, but then you freeze, slowly, and you start to think that maybe it wouldn't have been that bad. Maybe your life was worth screwing some old guy."

She was crying in earnest now, and Trey thought his heart would break with hers.

"I was waiting for permission to grow up. I didn't deserve it. I was acting like a child when I ran away."

"It was a jail break. Rebecca, you were trying to get out of a kind of prison."

"When she called, she said I hadn't fooled anyone, and she knew I was in Austin. 'That bitch Patricia didn't invite you to her wedding.' I hung up the phone, and I had to go. Just go, anywhere. I wasn't thinking straight. It was crazy."

"You're allowed to have moments of craziness. Everyone does." God knew he had. Stupid, stupid moments that could have gotten him killed. Hanging out with other kids who knew they were flunking out.

Drinking moonshine. Walking down the center line of a highway.

Rebecca hadn't been thinking straight, but she hadn't intended to run out of gas with an ice storm on the horizon. He'd practically dared the universe to kill him.

"You've lived to tell the tale, Rebecca. You've got a chance now to live your life, your way. I know you'll grab that with both hands."

It was more than he'd done. He'd stayed in one spot. Scared every time his brain let him down, he'd stuck to the undemanding life he'd stumbled into. Spreading mulch. Pulling weeds. Eating instant soup from the convenience store that he could see from his apartment, the one he couldn't get lost walking to.

Ten years later, he owned his own trucks and employed a dozen men, but he was still that same guy, stuck where life had dropped him.

But Rebecca Cargill, she was special. Ten years from now, she would be living her own life, free from her mother's demands. That life was starting here. He was witnessing a new beginning, her independence emerging as he sheltered her in his arms.

God, how he wanted her. He, who never left his safety zone, wanted her, a woman who could choose to go anywhere and be anything she wanted, after they survived this storm.

After they spent this night together.

He could seduce her. When she'd first regained consciousness, she'd kissed him with a hunger that could burn them both up. It would be a pleasure to change the tone of these caresses. He could touch her in a way that would ignite the flames that simmered inside her. They'd have a night to remember, because the one thing he'd never had to doubt about himself was that women enjoyed him in bed. But outside of bed...

There was a reason he'd never come home. As one of the top football players in the nation, the city of Austin had known his name. The whole town had been disappointed in him, their native son. He hadn't wanted to face that, so he'd waited a decade for the city to forget him. He couldn't drag Rebecca into a life with a man that cowardly.

He hadn't been good enough for any other girlfriend in his own estimation. Not good enough for Elaine, who'd passed the bar while he'd only passed high school. Not good enough for Bonnie, who'd loved to throw a party, always bringing in new people, new faces, too many for him to learn, too confusing for him to mingle with. Not good enough for Robin, who'd been able to teach anyone to read piano music. Anyone but him. He'd pretended he wasn't even trying when she'd pulled him over to the piano bench to show him how to play.

What made him think he'd ever be good enough for Rebecca Cargill, whose life lay before her, pure potential?

But God above, he could make her happy for one night.

The temptation was too much. He dropped one last kiss on her bare, delicious shoulder, unzipped the sleeping bag and left.

* * *

"Where are you going?"

Becky was mortified. Trey was leaving her, going into the dangerous, freezing outdoors. What had she done? What had she said?

"I need to make you a fire," he said, blanket wrapped around him as he stomped into his boots. "I have to gather the wood before it storms again."

"It's too dark. What if you get hurt? How would I help you?" She sat up in the sleeping bag, her face filling the circular opening, tracking his every move as if she could jump up and stop him.

"I won't get hurt. I've got a flashlight, and we've got mesquite trees right here. I'm just going to pick up what wood is already on the ground."

She felt like a child who was being left alone to face the monsters under the bed. Her monster was the cold wind, and it was forcing its way into the cabin, driving through the walls. Without Trey to keep it at bay, it would get her.

"I'll be right outside the door," he said, bending to scoop his sheepskin coat off the floor.

"Don't go, please. We're plenty warm. We don't need a fire." She sounded like a child, petulant and pleading.

He smacked the coat against the cabin wall, sending ice crystals showering to the floor. "We need a goddamned fire. Our clothes are frozen." He picked up a smaller item from the pile of clothes, and closed his fist around it. It made a slight noise, like a piece of tissue paper crumpling.

He hurled it at the wall, the blanket falling from his

shoulder. In the moonlight, she saw his arm muscles flex in chiseled relief, the power in his throw impressive and intimidating.

But he didn't leave. One by one, he smacked each item of clothing against the wall to shake off its ice, then hung it on a peg or nail. There was a neat row of wooden pegs to the right of the fireplace, but there were also random nails driven in various places, no doubt hammered there over the years to serve as hooks for hunting or fishing gear.

The item he'd hurled against the wall, she saw, was plaid boxer shorts. Her bra, pink and plain, hung on the nail next to them. The sight should have made her blush.

She bit her lip. The sleeping bag was already less warm without Trey by her side.

"I thought it was strictly survival," she said, "and no clothing was the best way to stay warm."

"It is. It was." He crouched by the hearth and twisted to look up the chimney, checking that it was clear. The blanket shifted with his moves, and she knew it wasn't keeping his body heat in very well. She could hardly stand to watch. He would freeze.

She didn't want him to freeze. It was painful, the way the muscles shook. It was scary, the way feet and hands lost all sensation. She didn't want him to go through it.

"Get back in the sleeping bag," she pleaded. "We don't need our clothes."

"Yes, damn it all to hell, we do." He glared at her in the patchy moonlight. "This closeness is killing me, Rebecca, because it's not close enough. I want to touch you. I want to be inside you. Damn it, if we had clothes, a frigging pair of boxer shorts, anything—" He cut himself off.

She stared at him. His breaths came loudly, harsh in the cold air, puffs of vapor disappearing as quickly as he breathed each one out. He closed his eyes and dropped his head.

"I didn't mean to say that." He grit the words out through his clenched jaw.

He didn't want to have sex with her. Her touch had driven him out into the cold.

"I'm sorry," she said, in a small voice. "I won't touch you. I'll try not to move at all. Please, don't freeze to death because of me. I'll be good."

"You'll be good?" He looked away from her and laughed, a short sound with no humor. "Rebecca, it takes two. You'll be good, but I'll try to change your mind. I'll succeed. We'll make love."

Yes, let's make love.

The thought was immediate, and true. Now she was the one who breathed harshly into the cabin.

Trey took one look at her face and left the cabin, slamming the door behind him.

Chapter Eight

The wood was too wet too burn.

Rebecca watched Trey spread the sticks and branches out on the floor, much as he'd spread their clothes on the wall. He'd said it might dry enough for them to get a fire started in the morning.

When he finished, he stayed crouched before the fireplace in the Navajo blanket, brooding at the cold hearth as if it had dancing flames to ponder.

She'd had enough time to ponder things herself after he'd stomped out the door, and she'd reached two conclusions. First, after hours of holding her nude body, he'd apparently felt some sexual urges toward her, and they'd horrified him so much, he was risking hypothermia to avoid her touch.

Second, she'd realized that when he was out of her sight for more than a minute, she was irrationally petrified that she would die. She knew that wasn't healthy, but the bottom line was that she'd been close to dying before he'd found her. Now that Trey was here, she was alive. It was unfortunate for him that he found her so repulsive, because she was going to stick to him like glue, anyway.

"Are you going to come back in the sleeping bag now?" she asked.

"In a minute."

"Come in now, and we'll trade places."

That got his attention. "You can't spend the night in this blanket, not even for a short time. It's not warm enough for me, or else I'd use it. Look, Rebecca, you don't have to be afraid of me. I say things without thinking, but I don't have any problem controlling myself. Forget that part about me trying to change your mind. I won't try to seduce you, and I'd never force you to do anything."

"Okay, fine." He didn't need to keep telling her how much he didn't want to touch her. "I need to use the blanket for something else, if you know what I mean."

He frowned at her for a moment, until understanding dawned. "I don't think it's a good idea for you to go outside on your own."

"You made me drink a canteen and a bottle of water. I don't have an option."

He sighed and got to his feet. She wriggled to sit up in the sleeping bag. He was so darned tall, that only put her face above his knee.

He announced his plan. "We'll stay as warm as we can under this blanket together. We'll just step onto the porch. Half the boards are missing, so you can find a spot—"

"No way. I'm not that fragile."

"I'm not risking it."

"You think you're going to stand next to me?" The idea was outrageous.

"I won't look." He had the nerve to act like she was the one being unreasonable.

"Trey! I'm not going to be able to go if you're standing there."

"This is survival. You can't stay warm in the sleeping bag by yourself. I'm not sending you out there alone in a blanket."

This was it, a new all-time low in her life of being obedient. She would have to pee where she was told.

To heck with being good; she let herself get mad. "Actually, I've been staying warm in this sleeping bag all by myself while you've been out there gathering wood to get away from my repulsive, non-teenager-like body. I've had a lot to drink and eat, and I'm feeling much stronger. This entire debate is ridiculous. Maybe little Becky would put up with this, but Rebecca won't." She unzipped the sleeping bag and stood tall.

Okay, it was the first time she'd actually ever stood next to him, and she hadn't realized just how huge the guy was. Still, she had righteous indignation on her side. She yanked the blanket from around his body and wrapped it around herself. Head high, she opened the cabin door.

"Your boots!" he hollered at her.

"Keep the sleeping bag warm." She slammed the door behind her.

Holy moly, it was cold outside. She two steps to the nearest gaping hole in the porch and quickly took care of business. Thirty seconds, max, was all she was outside, but that was long enough to know he'd been right about the boots. Her feet were freezing on the planks of the porch, so she ran inside.

He was holding the flap of the sleeping bag open. She ditched the blanket and dove inside, plastering every square inch of her body to his. All thoughts of sex and modesty were irrelevant.

"Oh my gosh, it's cold out there."

"Told you so." He sounded grumpy and just a little bit arrogant, but the fact that he was holding her made her heart hurt less.

"Fine," she said generously. "You were right. My feet are frozen."

He didn't laugh at that, but slid her up his body until he could reach her foot with his hand. He squeezed gently. "I'm afraid you might have frostbite."

"They're warming up already. All of me is warming up. I think I'm just normal cold, not cold cold."

"I think you're right."

"It's a relief to just be normal cold." She owed it all to him, and she'd never, ever forget that. "Thank you."

Because he'd slid her high enough to reach her feet, her head was above his. She could have tucked the top of his head under her chin the way he'd been tucking hers, so she kissed his forehead gratefully, and she did.

The new position placed his mouth just above her breasts.

"Are we back to the thank-yous? You really need to get those out of your system." He said it lightly, with mock grumpiness, but his breath fanned across the top of her breasts as he spoke, and she couldn't laugh.

"Rebecca," he said, so quietly she might have imagined it, but she felt his breath with each syllable. He put his hands on her hips and drew her back down until they were once more face-to-face, the way they'd started.

This time, Rebecca paid attention to where and how they touched. Nose to nose, they were nearly shoulder to shoulder, and her arm wrapped around him naturally. Her feet tangled with his calves, but the lower half of his body did not touch her. She realized he'd been keeping their distance with a hand on her hip, or on her knee, or by rolling away, the entire time. She wriggled forward, and although his hand was on her hip, he did not stop her from getting too close.

Against her thigh, she felt him. She was no expert, none at all, but she'd read the educational books, and knew men got erections. She'd read novels, and knew about velvet over steel. That was surely what she was feeling, heavy against her thigh, warmer than all the other warm skin on his body.

Her lower belly reacted with something very like a shiver, and she nestled closer to him, the tips of her breasts flattening against his chest. In the dim light, she saw his eyelids close halfway, as if they were heavy with sleep, but otherwise, he stayed very, very still.

"I thought you didn't want to have sex with me," she whispered.

"I didn't say that. I know I didn't say that, because I've never had that thought."

Confusion warred with the sweet sensation of being desirable. "Then are you committed to someone? Do you have a girlfriend?"

"No. It just wouldn't be a good idea. You're about to start a whole new chapter in your life. Starting tomorrow, you've got a lot of thinking to do. You have to decide where you're going from here."

"Maybe I've decided the first thing I want to do is have sex with you." She couldn't believe how easily she said those words. The darkness gave her courage, perhaps, although she wished she could see his face better.

"You don't know me."

"I know so much about you. You saved me."

"I think there might be a little bit of that syndrome—what is it called?"

"Stockholm syndrome?"

He chuckled, breaking the tension, and gave her hip a playful push. "No, that's when you fall in love with your kidnapper. Nightingale, that's the one."

She wrinkled her nose. "Florence Nightingale? Falling in love with your nurse?"

"With whatever person saved you." He spoke kindly, tucking her hair behind her ear. "I don't need sex from a woman who'd really just be saying thank you. You'd regret it in the morning."

She let that sink in. It sounded so reasonable. She *was* grateful to him for saving her.

Into the silence, Trey spoke with authority. "Get some sleep. You're exhausted."

Frowning, she didn't object when he rolled her away with a gentle push. She turned her back to him, so they were spooning in the sleeping bag—except, of course, he kept his hand at her waist and he scooted his hips

back, away from the curve of her backside. It wasn't
what she wanted.

Tomorrow, they'd build a fire and dry their clothes.
They'd drive the ATV back to the house. She wondered
if his family would still be there, the aunt and the uncle.
And then the lightbulb went off in her head.

"You're wrong, Trey." She propped herself awk-
wardly on her elbow and twisted her face toward his,
although it was dark. "What if your uncle had found
me? Do you think I'd be so grateful that I'd want to
have sex with him? What about your cousin Emily?
Do you think if she'd come riding up on that ATV, I'd
suddenly have a thing for her? That Nightingale syndrome is an insult. You're saying I'd want to be with
any person who found me."

He rubbed his jaw, so heavy with stubble that she
could hear the abrasion in the dark. "What if another
cowboy found you? A guy your age, blond, good-
looking?"

He had no clue, this man she'd gotten to know so
well. She frowned at him and hoped he could see it.
"That all depends. When I tell him about my life, does
he listen, or does he interrupt? When I'm mad at my
own stupidity, does he tell me I'm a good survivor,
or does he warn me not to do it again? Look, I'm not
going to beg you to have sex with me, but don't insult
me. I know what I want, and I want you, Trey Waterson, not just any old rescuer."

Tears were blurring her eyes, not that there was
much to see in the night, but then one plopped on Trey's
arm, so she knew he was aware. "And just so you know,

I'm not crying because I'm sad. I'm so *damned* frustrated with you. I couldn't have sex with you now if I wanted to, I'm so mad. So good night."

And then she turned her back to him once more, and dropped her head onto his arm to use as a pillow.

She was determined not to cry in the arms of the man who refused to be her lover.

Trey was stunned.

Rebecca was furious with him, lying against him with a tension he could feel humming along the length of her body.

But he felt a different emotion entirely. She'd slayed him. She'd hovered over him in the dark, and shown him what a fool he was with a few choice words. She was no innocent babe, unsure of the world. She knew herself, and she knew him, and he'd never been so wrong before.

She wanted him, and he was starving for her.

"Rebecca," he murmured, and he kissed her perfect ear. He inhaled the warmth of her neck, exposed as it was while she lay with her back to him. He tasted the skin of her shoulder, savoring it, saying her name, apology in every syllable. "Rebecca, Rebecca."

He moved his hand to cup her breast, holding its soft weight, learning her every dimension. "I didn't know how you felt until you told me. I want you, too. I know you, too."

He'd be her lover, because she'd demanded it. He wasn't surprised when she turned toward him and pressed him flat on his back. In the safety of their sleeping bag, she lay atop him, chest pressed to chest, her knees on either side of his hips.

She slid slowly up the length of him, and exhaled shakily. Sexily. Then she moved again, gliding up his length, and he sensed she was too close to the edge already. He gripped her hips to stop her motion.

As she leaned over him, she spoke in his ear, intimate words between lovers. "I've changed my mind, Trey. This isn't going to be sex. This is making love. Emotional, involved, sloppy lovemaking, where I tell you how much I love you. I know there's some hero worship in there, but I really don't care, because my heart wants you even more than my body does. We're alive, Trey, and we fit together. You know we do. Let's make love. Right. Now."

He'd already positioned her. Controlling her hips with his hands, he brought her down on him as he thrust himself into her. Her swift intake of breath was one of surprise; the small sound that escaped her throat told him the rest. The significance almost overwhelmed him, but knowing that she'd chosen him increased his passion, this driving need to make her his. *Her first, her first, her first time—*

He spent himself swiftly, not wanting to cause her more pain, and then it was his turn to speak, to murmur in her ear. With his fingers, he searched for the spot that would bring her pleasure as he held his body motionless inside her. He didn't have to censor himself or be careful about what he said, because he wanted her to hear the truth. As his fingers circled and her excitement built, he told her she was perfect and he was happy, so happy, to be with her, that she felt amazing and she *was* amazing. As she reached her peak, he told her how beautiful it was because he was still inside her and felt it all.

And then, there was silence. He held her and was held by her, and their breathing slowed. They kept each other warm.

With the side of her face pressed to his throat, he could feel the tickle of her eyelashes as she blinked. "Close your eyes, sweetheart. Go to sleep."

"I don't want to close my eyes. I knew when I was standing by that tree that if I fell asleep, I would never wake up."

He stroked her hair. "I promise you, you'll see the morning. As long as we're together, Rebecca, we'll survive. Close your eyes, and rest."

Chapter Nine

The fire was going strong, burning brightly as the early-morning light poured into the cabin along with the cold air. The wood hadn't dried much overnight, but Trey had brought an artificial fire starter that had ignited the first piece. Once that blazed, Trey had been able to carefully add one damp piece after another, building the fire steadily. The wet wood hissed steam, but it also provided the heat they needed, as long as Trey went about it methodically, carefully. He could not rush.

"Could you hurry that up a little bit? I need to use the blanket, if you know what I mean."

Trey smiled at Rebecca's words. For a woman who'd been raised to be patient and silent, she sure was eager and energetic around him.

"If you want it, come and get it," he said. The fire would keep him warm enough for a few minutes. He was rewarded with his first good look at his naked Rebecca, all smooth skin and tousled hair, as she bounded from the sleeping bag to him. The smile on her face stole his attention from her shapely legs. She snatched the blanket from around his shoulders and whisked it around her own, but she didn't turn to the door immediately.

Trey realized she was checking him out, too, getting her first look at his body in the daylight. He stayed as he was, crouched on one knee, and tossed another stick on the fire. His bent thigh, he knew, was blocking some of what she was probably curious to view, but as he slid a glance at her, she was smiling.

It turned out that his innocent porcelain angel could execute an excellent wolf whistle. "I sure did get a good-looking cowboy."

As she turned and walked out the door, he yelled "Boots" over his shoulder.

"I know. I'm a fast learner." She stomped them on, and left.

A good-looking cowboy. Trey rubbed his forehead, and fed the fire. He wasn't a damned cowboy. He was a landscaper in a medium-sized town in Oklahoma. He planted trees and maintained some nice plants around office buildings.

Worse, he was a landscaper who had to hire someone else to total the checks and send out the bills, because the boy who'd once aced calculus couldn't keep a simple ledger. He was a landscaper who asked each new client to write their address for him on their contract. He rode in the passenger seat of his own trucks, and handed the written address to whichever crew member he'd put in the role of redneck chauffeur.

He was less than a landscaper.

Yet he'd taken an irreversible step with Rebecca last night. He'd seen the evidence of her virginity on his body this morning, and the emotions had hit him square in the chest. He'd felt honored. Responsible. But mostly, possessive. Insanely possessive, in the most primitive way, for she was his woman, and his alone. The idea of another man touching what only he had touched sent a fighting dose of adrenaline through his system.

That was a problem. He and Rebecca would break up one day. There would be no forever for her with a man like him. The humiliation of his handicaps was not to be shared. Given their circumstances and geography, he and Rebecca would part company sooner rather than later.

If he was any kind of decent man, he'd stop sleeping with her and start acting like the distant friend—no more—that he'd inevitably end up being.

"It's starting to snow out there," Rebecca said as she came back inside. "Do you think it will stick? We could have a white Christmas." She was all sunshine on this snowy day, an early Christmas gift wrapped in a Navajo blanket.

This break up was going to hurt when it happened. Trey knew it would hurt in a way he'd never get over.

She stayed near the door. "Would you help me with my boots?"

The temperature in the cabin was probably still at freezing, except directly in front of the fire. Her blanket dipped and slipped open as he hauled off one of her boots. Her breast was exposed for a moment, pure and luscious, before it was hidden by the colorful blanket once more.

Did his body respond in the freezing cold? With a vengeance.

Oblivious, smiling, Rebecca opened the blanket and invited him in. As she closed her arms around his neck, with the corners of the blanket tight in her fists, she kissed him as she had the first time, with a raw, open-mouthed hunger. He'd broken off that kiss before, but he couldn't now. This was his woman, and she wanted him, and by God, he'd worry about tomorrow when tomorrow came.

Still kissing, he backed her toward the sleeping bag, which he'd dragged closer to the fire. When her feet touched it, she dropped the blanket, and they both slid into the familiar warmth. She snuggled her bare body up to his, as familiar with him as he was with her after their hours and hours of togetherness.

There was something so primal about it, very Adam and Eve, innocent and naked, just the two of them in this log cabin. He was male, she was female, and everything about her was a pleasure to him, from her face to her voice, from her body to her laugh.

She pushed his hair back with her fingers and looked at him with those brown doe eyes. "It only hurts the first time, right?"

"That's what I've heard."

"You don't know?" Her eyes widened, and then she started raining little kisses from one corner of his mouth to the other. "I'm your first *first*. I am, aren't I?"

"Rebecca, you're my first everything."

He stopped himself. He'd been about to say all kinds of things. The words were lined up, ready to pour out.

You're the first good reason I've had to want to face the day. You're the first woman I've wanted to love.

It was an agony to hold it in, but he would not tell her he loved her when he knew he would leave her.

"What do you mean, your first?" she whispered, laying him back, prowling over him. She bit her lip, excited and anxious at once for what they were about to do—for they were, with a certainty, about to come together once more. It was as inevitable as breathing. It had been from the first moment he'd held her, Trey realized.

"There's never been another like you," he said, his back to the hard planks of the floor as Rebecca moved on top of him once more. "There never will be."

Together, they learned that the second time involved some physical tenderness. Rebecca had been dismayed that her body was delicate, because her desire was undeniable. Trey had led them to completion with more gentleness than he'd known he possessed, and they'd finished breathless and satisfied. The tenderness of the second time, Trey knew, had been as much in his heart as her body. It would be seared in his memory. He might forget everything else, but never that.

The silence they shared in each other's arms was broken by the chop of a helicopter's blades, coming to take them away.

The dusting of Texas snow turned into a blizzard under the helicopter's blades, flakes and ice and dirt flying in all directions, pelting them with fury.

Fury. That was what Trey was feeling. The arrival

of the helicopter had made Rebecca distressed, and that made him angry. She'd rushed to get dressed, insisting on wearing her underpants, although they'd begun thawing and were now both cold and damp. The destroyed cashmere cardigan was the most wet item of them all, yet she'd put it on and tried to hold it closed.

Trey had pulled the cardigan off her arms and tossed it in the fire, then dressed her in his plaid Western shirt. The material was thinner but far more dry, and it reached nearly to her knees, which satisfied her sense of modesty. She'd worn the Navajo blanket instead of her wet coat. He'd worn his jeans and wrapped the foil-backed thermal blanket around himself, and they'd left everything else behind in the cabin.

At the first blast of dirt and ice, Trey had cursed himself for leaving the goggles. As Rebecca bent her head and shaded her eyes with her hands, Trey hated his sorry excuse of a brain, which had let him down once more—and Rebecca, too.

He should have foreseen that a helicopter would arrive. He'd told his cousin to call the sheriff, something that had completely slipped his mind until now. The ice storm had stopped, the darkness had lifted, their fire had created smoke. Therefore, the helicopter had come. Why couldn't he predict these things?

The helicopter wasn't painted with the sheriff's office colors, though. It was Texas Rescue and Relief's logo that was emblazoned on the side. Texas Rescue was the organization that his brother volunteered with as a fireman. Luke's new wife did something with them, too, but damn if Trey could remember what. He didn't care. He was angry with Texas Rescue, because they were literally taking Rebecca away.

A man had descended with a metal basket. He was dressed like an astronaut in a full helmet and orange jumpsuit, but he kept giving them hearty, thumbs-up gestures. Trey felt like returning the hand gesture with a different one of his own.

He would have gotten Rebecca home safely. If they'd only given him some time, he could have completed the rescue. The fire that he'd just doused had been going strong. Their clothes had been drying. He would have waited one more night, letting Rebecca get stronger, and then he would have refilled the ATV with the spare gas can before beginning the return drive over the land he knew like the back of his hand. Rebecca would have ridden behind him, and his own body would have blocked the cold wind for her.

But his plan took time. Like building a fire with damp wood, each piece of his plan had to be executed step-by-step. It was a pace that worked for him.

But Trey knew, as he'd known since he'd been un-ceremoniously booted out of Oklahoma Tech, that the world moved at a faster pace.

Rebecca had already disappeared into the helicop-ter, and the astronaut was holding the basket steady for Trey to climb in. Once inside the helicopter, the pace only quickened. The astronaut removed his helmet, stuck a thermometer in Rebecca's mouth and clipped a white plastic device on Trey's finger. After things beeped, he switched them around, popping fresh plastic on the thermometer for Trey, clipping the white cube on Rebecca's finger.

Then he turned to Trey and stuck his hand in front of his face. "How many fingers am I holding up?" he shouted over the relentless thumping of the rotor blades.

Alarm raced through Trey. They were going to start all this crap again, how many fingers, look up, look to the left, follow my finger with your eyes. There was nothing wrong with his eyes, there'd never been anything wrong with his eyes, just a little double vision after a hit during practice.

"How many fingers?" the man shouted again.

"Four, goddammit."

"Jeez, Trey, nice to see you, too. Don't take my head off." Then he turned to Rebecca and asked her the same.

The astronaut knew him.

That sick sweat threatened. Trey rolled his shoulders and tried to concentrate on the man's face. If he'd just hold still. If he'd just give Trey a minute to place his face—but he was shouting numbers he read off the white cube cheerfully, as if Trey would be glad to hear them, all while packing up equipment, pulling a microphone from a clip in the roof, talking to the pilot as he took Rebecca's temperature a second time. The engine roared, the helicopter banked, and instead of ranch land below them, city buildings and highways filled the window.

Somehow, Trey had assumed they were flying back to the ranch house. Foolish.

He could only focus on one thing at a time, and the only thing he gave a damn about was Rebecca. She looked at him, and smiled her strained, driver's license smile.

Trey unbuckled his seat belt and moved to her side.

"You done?" he asked the astronaut, but it wasn't really a question. He unbuckled Rebecca's seat belt and pulled her into his lap, blanket and all.

The other man shot him a look that Trey returned evenly. *This is the way it's going to be.*

The man got the message. He pulled the seat belt's webbing out another few feet, then buckled it around Trey and Rebecca, both. "You won't mind if I buckle my patients in. I just got my rescue swimmer's certification. I'm not losing it for you, Waterson. And, ma'am, since your bodyguard doesn't seem inclined to introduce us, I'm Zach Bishop. Pleased to meet you."

Zach Bishop. Of course, Trey knew Zach Bishop. Trey's senior year, Zach had been a freshman on the football team. He'd thought he was the best wide receiver in the state. He wasn't, but he was good, so Trey had thrown more than a few touchdown passes his way. Just to remind the cocky freshman who was behind those scores, Trey would unleash his full, NFL-worthy strength at him during practice, and throw the ball so hard that it would knock Zach on his ass when he caught it.

He realized now why Zach was grinning at him. They had a history, a rivalry and grudging respect, one Trey had forgotten for ten years.

He looked at Rebecca's face, still new to him, and

tried to memorize it. Would she be erased from his consciousness for ten years? Would he run into her someday, and wonder why this sweet brunette acted like she knew him?

The thought made his gut churn. He couldn't allow it to happen. He wanted those memories of their first time, and their second. If he had to keep her beside him and look at her every single day to keep that memory fresh, then that was what he'd do.

Until she wanted to move in, settle down, have children. Then he'd have to let her go.

Chapter Ten

Rebecca Cargill had never been in a hospital before. She hated it.

Her entire twenty-four years had been spent wrapped in a pink puffy safety bubble. She'd never broken a bone and needed a cast, because she'd never climbed a tree. She'd never stepped on broken glass and needed stitches, because she'd never gone outside without her white lace socks and black patent Mary Janes. She'd gotten bronchitis once, the year she'd been sent to an exclusive all-girl boarding school courtesy of Papa Maynard, Mother's fourth husband. A physician had come to her dormitory and prescribed an antibiotic. The floor mistress had administered it as she plumped little Becky Cargill's precious pillows twice a day.

The helicopter had landed on the roof of the hospital, and the wind from the rotors had buffeted Rebecca every which way as she was taken out of Trey's arms and placed on an empty stretcher. She'd been swaddled in white blankets and held down with seat belts across her legs and waist and shoulders, and then six people had run along the side of her stretcher as they rushed her away like she was on a television drama, playing the patient who was about to die.

Maybe she was. Maybe she was suffering from some aftereffects of her freezing, and didn't know it. Everyone was so serious, so urgent. They rolled her into an elevator, and from there into a room with medical equipment hanging on its walls. Some of it she could identify, like oxygen masks, and some of it she could read, like "defibrillator," but most of it was an array of ominous stainless steel and black plastic, waiting for a life to be in danger.

Was it hers?

It could be. Trey was not here, and without him, she could die. In this hospital, the thought didn't seem so irrational.

A woman in scrubs informed her they were going to take some vitals, and then she unsnapped the shirt Rebecca had borrowed from Trey and stuck round electrodes on Rebecca's chest, pushing one breast aside a bit to stick a circle on her rib. The television screen over the stretcher started to display a bright green zigzag, and the telltale beep that Rebecca recognized from every medical movie started tracking her heartbeat.

Rebecca wondered if the number one hundred and twenty was her pulse, but before she could ask, another woman in scrubs wiped her elbow crease with cold alcohol and inserted a needle to start an IV. The bag of clear fluid, hanging from its silver hook, dripped steadily into the tube that disappeared into her arm. *Sodium Chloride*, it read.

Little Becky was frightened into silence, but Rebecca, who had the confidence to tell a man when he was wrong, asked the nurse a question. "What kind of medicine is that?"

"Oh, it's nothing. Just a precaution for dehydration." She stuck a wide piece of clear plastic over the crease of Rebecca's elbow. Rebecca kept her arm completely straight, afraid to move and dislodge the needle.

Trey had said she was dehydrated. He'd made her drink more than she'd wanted to. Had he known how sick she was? But she wasn't getting water now. She was getting sodium chloride, which the nurse said was nothing. She didn't trust the nurse; *nothing* wouldn't have a name.

She trusted Trey. She needed him to keep her warm and safe, but he wasn't here. The hospital wouldn't have kept him, she supposed, because there was nothing wrong with him. He hadn't frozen slowly in the cold. The helicopter had dropped her off at the hospital, but maybe it had taken Trey somewhere else, since he wasn't sick.

"My arm is cold." The panic was threatening to make itself heard in her voice. She could feel a creeping coldness in her arm, spreading deep under her skin.

The nurse patted her hand. "Yes, sometimes you can feel the IV going in. It's okay. The doctor will be in shortly."

The last two people left, and shut the door.

Rebecca lay in the bed, and stared at the door. It had one lone holiday decoration, a plastic cling in the shape of a snowflake. She stared at the imitation ice crystal as her ECG machine beeped.

Her shoulder started to hurt from holding it at a funny angle to keep her arm straight, but she didn't dare move with the needle stuck in her. They were putting a cold liquid inside her, when she never wanted to be cold again.

Trey!

No wonder people dreaded going to the hospital. She'd never felt so alone…except for the time she'd been clinging to a tree in the middle of nowhere. Her feet had frozen, minute by minute.

The ECG beeped faster. Rebecca flexed her feet. They were still there, but the seat belt kept her from moving her legs. They'd released the one across her shoulders and the one across her middle, but no one had done anything to her feet.

She held still, legs strapped in place. Needle in her arm. Wires coming out of the shirt from the stickers on her chest.

"Trey!"

She shouted his name, but he was not coming in the door this time. He was not here.

"Trey," she said quietly, more of a wish than a cry for help.

The door opened a few inches, and yet another woman in scrubs stuck her head in. This one was Rebecca's age, with brown hair in a high ponytail. "Hi. Did you need something?"

Rebecca swallowed. She couldn't think of the right sentence, only the kind of stilted phrases her mother had drilled into her head. *Would you please inform Mr. Waterson that Miss Cargill would like to see him?*

The woman glanced at the ECG and looked back at Rebecca. She came all the way into the room. "You don't look very comfortable. Is your IV bothering you?"

She flicked open the buckle on the leg seat belt as she walked up to Rebecca's side and placed her hand on her arm.

"Careful, please," Rebecca said quickly. "I don't want to wiggle the needle."

"There's no needle in there. They slide it out and leave a flexible tube in its place. You can bend your arm. Try it."

Rebecca was so relieved, she could have kissed the woman.

Florence Nightingale syndrome, she could hear Trey say.

I don't mean kiss her like that, Trey. Get your mind out of the gutter.

Oh, yes. She was bold and spunky when she talked to Trey, but she was still good little Becky everywhere else. She missed Trey intensely.

"You're allowed to have one person in the room with you," the woman said. "Is there someone in the waiting room I could get for you?"

"Trey Waterson. Except, I don't know if he's here or not."

"Trey? Okay, I'll go see if there is a Trey in the waiting room."

The minutes ticked by, measured by the rapid beep of the ECG machine.

The ponytail lady came back into the room. "There's

no one named Trey, but there's a woman out there who'd like to see you. Shall I send her in?"

Rebecca froze, and felt a new kind of cold, one she dreaded as much as any other she'd felt in Texas.

Her mother had arrived.

She lay there for a moment, obedient little Becky, and then she sat up. If Trey was not here, then she'd go find him. He was the only person in the world she trusted.

She started peeling the round circles off her chest, tossing the offensive pieces of plastic onto the stretcher, but she remembered her manners and smiled sweetly. "Thank you, but I do not wish to see that woman. It was very kind of you to check the waiting room, but I'm afraid I must be going now."

Somewhere in the back of her mind, she knew her behavior was irrational. She wouldn't do anything dangerous this time. She wouldn't take an ATV into the wilderness in an ice storm. She'd just use her credit card to rent another car, and she'd go back to the ranch and find Trey. Hopefully, she'd get there before her mother tracked her down.

If she could just find Trey—

The woman stopped Rebecca by placing a hand over hers. "Just a minute. I'll help you take the rest of those off. But first, I want you to know that nobody will come into this room without your permission. Only hospital personnel are allowed. You're safe." True to her word, she removed the rest of the electrodes.

"Second, I want you to stay in this safe room until the doctor can see you. You were assigned to Dr.

Brown, but she's got a patient from a car accident who's taking all her time. I'm going to get Dr. MacDowell to see you instead."

Trey recognized Dr. MacDowell immediately. He was Jamie, the youngest of the three MacDowell brothers who had played football for Trey's high school. The MacDowell family owned the River Mack Ranch, which bordered the James Hill Ranch to the east.

Trey had known Jamie MacDowell his entire life, but he doubted he would have remembered him if Zach Bishop hadn't been on that helicopter. It sometimes happened that way. Trey was missing a memory—without knowing it, of course—and then someone like Zach from football would come along, and suddenly, all the football memories would be unlocked. The MacDowells had played football. Trey now remembered the MacDowells.

Jamie—Dr. MacDowell—wanted him to walk in a straight line, heel toe, heel toe.

"Would you like me to tell you who the President of the United States is, too?" Trey asked. He was sick of this routine.

"Been through this before, huh?" Jamie said. "Sobriety test by a police officer, or did a doctor ask you?"

"Does it matter?"

"As a matter of fact, it does."

Trey had no patience for this. He wanted to check on Rebecca. "A doctor."

"When?"

"College. Let's get on with it."

"I'm going to give you three items, and I want you to remember them. A house, an apple, an elephant. Can you say those back to me?"

"House, apple, elephant. Got it."

"Do you know what each of those things are?"

This was the part that always made Trey the most angry. He hated being treated like he was a moron. "Give me a break, Jamie. House, apple, elephant. Let's move on."

There was a knock at the door, and an attractive woman Rebecca's age stuck her head in the room. "Dr. MacDowell, can I interrupt you, please?"

Trey sat on the treatment table, feeling like a fool in a hospital gown. He'd give Jamie about two minutes more of this nonsense, and then he'd find Rebecca.

"Sorry about that, Trey." Jamie came back in the room, only to be yanked back out by the sleeve of his white coat. Trey heard the woman ask Jamie if his patient's name was Trey. An indistinct conversation followed.

Jamie returned, taking his stethoscope from around his neck and putting it in his ears. "Let me listen to you breathe."

It was awkward, having the pest baby brother of his neighbors listen to his heart. Not awkward like sharing a sleeping bag while naked, but awkward all the same.

Jamie put his stethoscope back around his neck. "Earlier, I asked you to remember some words. Can you repeat those items back to me?"

"House and apple."

Jamie put a plastic cone on the end of a flashlight and asked Trey to stick out his tongue to say, "ah."

Trey wasn't fooled. "I can stick out my tongue straight."

"Say, 'ah,' damn it, and stop being such a stubborn cuss."

"Ah."

"Great." Jamie tossed the plastic cone in the trash. "The nursing assistant was just telling me that your Aunt June is in the waiting room with someone else. One of your cousins, I assume."

What the hell was everyone doing at the hospital? Trey had already been worried about getting Rebecca home. Now he had to transport Aunt June and Emily, too. That was four people. His pickup truck only held three.

"Thanks for the update," he said. "Now I've got to drive four people home in a three-man truck."

Jamie crossed his arms over his chest. His white coat flared behind him like a cattleman's duster. "You came by helicopter, Trey. You don't have a pickup truck here."

Aw, hell. It was so damned obvious when he pointed it out.

Trey tried to play it off. "I need to get some sleep. It's been a long twenty-four hours."

"You could also be dehydrated." Jamie handed him a hospital cup with ounces marked on its side. "I want you to drink all thirty-two ounces, and then I want you to fill it up and drink it again. Slam it, like you just finished football practice. I've got to see my next patient, but I'll be back. Drink up."

Trey wanted to ask where Rebecca was. Hell, he wanted to demand to be taken to her. But if he'd ever needed a reminder of why he wasn't man enough for her, he'd just gotten it.

Rebecca, Rebecca. He remembered the taste of her shoulder as he'd murmured the apology. He'd misunderstood how much she wanted him then.

How could he explain why he couldn't keep her now?

Chapter Eleven

Trey paced the treatment room after putting on his dry-enough jeans and reliable cowboy boots. He turned the hospital gown around so that it opened down the front. It felt more like a shirt that way, one he just hadn't buttoned up.

Jamie MacDowell came back into the room, tossed his clipboard on the sink counter and sank into the room's vinyl chair. He looked hard at Trey for a moment.

Trey waited. Whatever Jamie had to say, it was serious. Whatever it was, Trey truly didn't care. He didn't do serious with doctors anymore. They were always serious when they told him they'd found nothing. His problems were his to deal with.

"I just saw the woman you rescued from the ice storm. She asked about you."

Trey suddenly cared a hell of a lot more. He'd been ready to hear something serious about himself, but this was about Rebecca. The morning's memory was still achingly fresh in his mind. *Honored. Responsible. Possessive.*

"Where is she?" Trey made a move toward the door, but Jamie held up his hand.

"Not so fast. You aren't her next of kin. I'm bound by all kinds of patient privacy acts here. But I've known you my entire life, and I know you aren't going to hurt her, so I'm going to ask you a favor. You have every right to turn me down."

Trey sat slowly on the edge of the bed. Physically, he'd never hurt Rebecca, but if he didn't put some distance between them immediately, he was going to break her heart when he left.

She was Jamie MacDowell's patient now, and he was a good man. The hospital itself was well-known. Rebecca would be okay from here on out. Trey ought to bow out gracefully, right here, right now, before things got any deeper.

"You're under no obligation to say yes, and I shouldn't be asking. Let me explain that Miss Cargill is on a very high state of alert, physically."

"What does that mean?"

"It's not all that unusual, given what she's been through. The body can stay in survival mode even after a person is safe. I'm planning on sending her home with a few days of Valium, just so she can get some sleep."

"She doesn't want to close her eyes," Trey said, more to himself than Jamie. She was afraid she'd never wake up—unless Trey was there to keep her from freezing. He understood.

Jamie continued explaining. "I could give her a little something now, a sedative or anxiety med to take the edge off, but I'd rather see her heart rate and other vital signs come off high alert on their own before I discharge her.

"She's asking for you. I'd say she's fixated on you, like you're necessary to her well-being. Again, not that unusual, given the fact that you saved her life. You've done your part, so you're under no obligation at all, but I'd like to see if having you around will lower her stress levels. Would you consider waiting with her in her room? Just sit there, keep her company?"

Trey didn't like the picture Jamie painted. A future broken heart was an abstract concept in the face of Rebecca's immediate distress. He'd have to worry about tomorrow some other time.

Trey stood. "What room is she in?"

"Hold up. One more thing. Is there any reason she has to fear your aunt June?"

The question was so preposterous, Trey was certain his faulty brain had missed something.

"The nursing assistant told her there was a woman in the waiting room who'd like to see her, and Miss Cargill started trying to leave. Urgently. She wanted to find you. I checked out the waiting room myself. It's your aunt June."

"Your nursing assistant must have gotten it wrong."

"The nursing assistant is my wife," Jamie said. "I trust her judgment."

Why would Rebecca be frightened that a woman was waiting to see her? Trey was shaking his head at Jamie when the answer broke through. *Her mother.* Rebecca must have thought her mother had come to get her.

Damn it. It wasn't like Trey had forgotten about her mother: the woman controlled her, and she was trying to send Rebecca off with a man in exchange for houses or jewels or some other money-related thing. Because it hadn't been an immediate concern while they were worried about shelter, he hadn't thought about it yet. Piece by piece, one step at a time—his brain hadn't focused on that particular piece of wood, so to speak.

"I know who Rebecca is worried about. I'll handle it."

"All right, then. I'll walk you to room three."

Trey left the room, but Jamie was only a couple of inches shorter than he was, so the young doctor easily kept pace as Trey headed down the row of numbered cubicles.

"I don't need an escort," Trey said, impatient, embarrassed.

"My ER. My patient. My rules. Wait with her until radiology comes to do the CT scan."

"What is she getting a CT scan for?"

"She's not. You are."

Trey stopped short. "For a stupid comment about a pickup truck? I told you, I'm tired. You said dehydrated."

"Trey," Jamie said, his voice very low in the public hallway, "you forgot the elephants."

"What?"

"House, apple, elephants. You've been examined before. Second injuries are generally more dangerous than the first. It could be nothing, or it could be an old injury, but it's possible you hit your head during that rescue and you just don't remember it. I've had people brought in here who didn't know they'd been in a car accident ten minutes prior."

"It's not a new injury." Trey forced the words out. "Nothing old, either. I've been told I'm normal a half-dozen times."

"Maybe so, but when you exhibit the symptoms of a possible brain bleed, you don't leave my ER until I check it out."

Trey crossed his arms over his chest again and glared at Jamie. MacDowell seemed unimpressed. Little brothers, whether his own or his neighbors', had always been pests.

"You always were a pain in the neck," Trey said, speaking the thought out loud without intending to. He refused to apologize. He wouldn't mutter his usual *I didn't mean to say that*. It was better to let Jamie think it was intentional instead of another case of forgetting elephants.

"Well, now I'm a pain in the neck with an MD after my name."

"Which means what?"

"Which means you're getting a CT scan. Quit fighting it."

Trey had no intention of fighting, and every intention of leaving. Jamie could fill out the paperwork for a patient who refused treatment. Trey didn't want to hear, one more time, that everything was normal.

But they were standing outside of room three. Trey would not turn and walk out of the hospital now.

Rebecca wanted him, so he'd stay awhile longer, and

he'd probably get another damned CT scan because he couldn't leave Rebecca here, not for any reason.

He turned the doorknob and left Jamie standing in the hall.

Rebecca watched the IV drip. She was sitting on the edge of the bed, toes grazing the tile floor, ready to jump up when the IV bag was empty, so she could get the tube taken out of her arm and get the heck out of this hospital.

Somehow, some way, she had to get back to the James Hill Ranch. Her rental car was already there, so she'd have to rent another one. She didn't care. She'd do whatever it took to get to Trey.

When she found him, she wanted to kill him. She imagined him in that ranch house, standing by that ginormous stone fireplace, waiting for her to show up once she was all better. She was going to show up, alright, and she was going to give him a piece of her mind. She was so angry at him for leaving her all alone, she would never speak to him again.

I couldn't have sex with you now if I wanted to, I'm so mad, she'd said last night. She meant it this time.

The door opened, and Trey walked in, denim below, bare-chested above, with the open flaps of a hospital gown trailing behind him.

He was the most beautiful sight she'd ever seen. She was standing and reaching for him without thinking about it, but he'd already reached her and was closing his arms around her. She clung to his neck, but her IV tubing stretched to its limit, so she lowered that arm and held on for dear life with the other.

"I missed you so much," she said, over and over, when what she'd planned to say was *How dare you leave me?* She wanted to kiss him, but she clung to him and buried the side of her face in his neck. "No one will tell me what's wrong with me, and my mother is waiting to take me away."

Trey stroked her hair and listened as she continued to babble on. "I know I'm supposed to be starting a new life, but this is my first time in a hospital and it's hard not to be silent after all these years, because I don't know these people, not like I know you. I didn't know where you were…"

He held her tightly against his chest. The sheer physical size of him was comforting to hang on to, and she ran out of things to say. Only then did he talk.

"Your mother isn't here. It's my aunt June in the waiting room. You won't see your mother without me." Trey pulled away from her far enough to hold her face in his hands.

He addressed only the issue of her mother, as if she hadn't gone through a list of worries. Rebecca realized that was the only issue that really had her scared. She was so relieved not to be alone. "You'll stay here? Just in case?"

"I'm not going anywhere. Hospitals like their rules, so they examined us separately, but we're together now." His gaze roamed from her eyes to her lips, and he gave her one soft kiss, but mostly, he cupped her face in his palms and looked at her.

"What is it?" she whispered, when she couldn't guess what his expression meant.

"I just want to memorize this pretty face."

And then they were kissing for real, openmouthed, hot and wet and hungry. He wanted her heat as much as she wanted his. It was a tremendous feeling, to think that she could be as important to him as he was to her.

She felt very near to tears, so she broke off the kiss to stand on tiptoe and whisper in his ear. "This probably sounds crazy, but I want to go back to the cabin."

"I know. It was easier."

There was a knock on the door, and Dr. MacDowell entered the room. Rebecca released her hold on Trey's neck. He was a little slower to release her, keeping her face in his hands, keeping his gaze on her face.

Dr. MacDowell sounded completely stunned. "Waterson—what are you—when I asked you to wait with her—"

Another quick knock, and the door opened again. Trey let go of her then, but only to sit on her bed and pull her down beside him, very close beside him. He put his arms around her, and Rebecca savored the shelter.

The ponytailed woman beamed at Rebecca. "Good, I see you've got your Trey."

Rebecca felt proud to have him by her side. *I'm not a loser without any friends,* she wanted to say. Until a few minutes ago, that was exactly what Rebecca had been, and this cheerful woman had been the only one who'd listened to her worries. "I'm sorry I made a scene. You've been very kind."

"If I'd been left alone in the ER, I'd have been yelling for my Jamie, believe me." She smiled at the doctor while she said it.

Rebecca's surprise must have shown on her face, because the woman hiked her thumb toward him and winked. "This is my husband, Jamie."

Dr. MacDowell introduced his wife to Trey, also to Rebecca's surprise. The men clearly knew each other. Trey stood when he was introduced to Kendry, a show of manners that somehow didn't surprise Rebecca, and then he spoke easily with the couple about living on neighboring ranches and playing football.

Rebecca listened to every word. Trey had been the quarterback at a high school, and Jamie had taken over once Trey had graduated. Kendry hadn't known them then, but she loved the high school games, and she told Trey this year's season had been great.

Rebecca watched the three of them chat, fascinated by Trey's history. Until this moment, he'd been simply hers. He'd materialized when she'd needed him most, and he'd been her exclusive property every moment since. She hadn't wondered what his life was like beyond her.

The MacDowells fascinated her, as well. They were a darling couple, the kind that Rebecca had witnessed now and then over the years. So much of her world had been spent with schoolmates whose fathers were on their third wives. Her mother's friends were women who vacationed with men they were not married to, but there had been exceptions. Rebecca had always noticed the exceptions.

She'd seen a millionaire get teary-eyed in the middle of raising a toast to his gray-haired wife. The Lexingtons' main home had been run by a married couple who'd worked together in the same mansion for decades. Rebecca knew true love existed, she just hadn't seen it up close very often, and she hadn't seen it in her own age group. The MacDowells couldn't take their eyes off each other. It was wonderful.

Kendry started to hook up Rebecca's ECG again in a far more discreet way than the first woman had done it.

"Now I see how you were able to get Dr. MacDowell to come see me when the other doctor was held up," Rebecca said.

Kendry winked. "I try not to throw my weight around, but sometimes, I just need to get things done."

Trey raised an eyebrow at Jamie. "Your ER? Your rules?"

Jamie shrugged. "Happy wife, happy life." He clapped Jamie on the shoulder and opened the door to leave. "You'll see."

All that new, friendly easiness left Trey's expression. Rebecca wondered where it went.

Sit up straight, Becky, for God's sake. Never behave like you think you are an imposition. Act like you belong here. Of course we should be included.

Her mother's advice was wrong. Wrong, wrong, wrong. Becky felt as if she was imposing—*no, not Becky; it's Rebecca now.* Rebecca felt as if she was imposing because she *was* imposing. She was an uninvited guest, no matter how gracious her hosts were being.

She had no choice but to accept their hospitality. She had absolutely nowhere to go, except the ranch house. She had nowhere she wanted to be, except with Trey, so she sat quietly, squashed in the backseat of Aunt June's car. She could do this, even without her mother. She'd done it so many times before.

Aunt June drove through the rain. Temperatures were above freezing, so the rain stayed wet and didn't turn to treacherous ice. June chatted away, pointing out a winery and raving about its gourmet olive oil as if Rebecca had come to Texas Hill Country to see the sights. At last, they passed the first of the simple crossbar gates that marked the highway that led to the James Hill Ranch.

"I don't mind telling you, young man," June began, glancing at Trey, "that it's a good thing your parents left on their own cruise after seeing Luke and Patricia off on theirs. When they check in, they'll find out you're already safe at the same time they hear you were missing overnight. You gave me enough gray hairs, charging out into that awful weather the way you did. I'm glad we'll spare your mother some."

She glanced in the rearview mirror at Rebecca. "How about you, honey? Do you need to tell your folks that you're safe now, or did they let you make a call from the hospital?"

Rebecca folded her hands in her lap. "Everything is just fine, thank you."

Trey was riding shotgun next to his aunt because he could not fit in the backseat. He was simply too large. In the cold light of day, Rebecca could see that he was at least six-four, with broad shoulders and long, strong legs that had carried her with long, strong strides across frozen ground. She loved the size of him, but it prevented him from sitting with her, so she was in the backseat, smiling politely at Emily's sincere attempts to carry on a conversation. Inside, however, her mother's warnings were relentless.

You must find out who really owns this house. Who was the last woman to stay here, and how long did she last? Why did she leave, or was she kicked out?

June and Emily had been the ones who'd insisted Rebecca come back to the house. Trey had been silent, wrapping the Navajo blanket around her before carrying her to the wheelchair so her feet wouldn't touch the ground. Her feet looked normal, but the next few days would tell how bad any frostbite had been. Her feet might blister. They might peel, and if they did, it would pass. But they might turn green or black, and if that happened, she was to return to the ER immediately.

June and Emily had practically given her the socks off their feet when they heard that. They really couldn't be nicer people. The problem was, they didn't own the house, and Trey, who hadn't said a word, lived in Oklahoma.

Rebecca felt uneasy. She and her mother had settled in with a man in Virginia once, in an area full of mansions and equestrian facilities. Rebecca had loved her new school and was looking forward to an entire semester in one place…maybe more. Maybe for a year or two, if Mother's boyfriend popped the question.

Then the boyfriend's mother had found out that he'd

let them move in, and Rebecca's mother had found out that although he lived there alone, he didn't own the house. His mother did. Becky and her mother had come home in the boyfriend's car from a shopping excursion to find their bags packed and lined up in the driveway.

Her mother had kept the car and the shopping bags, but never again did they move into a house without the owner's invitation. The real owner.

They were still a long way from the James Hill Ranch. Rebecca was smiling politely and worrying silently. Emily was telling her she'd already brought her suitcases in from her rental car, so she could just jump into a warm shower when they got home. June was describing all the catered wedding food that could be heated up without any problem at all.

Trey said, "A rescue swimmer."

Silence filled the little car.

I say things without thinking, Trey had told her in the dark. She'd thought he meant something different.

"Did you say swimmer, honey?" his aunt asked.

Trey cleared his throat and made a vague gesture out the window toward a distant barn. "Texas Rescue sent a rescue swimmer to get us. All this ice and snow and rain are going to cause flash floods and drownings. That's why they sent a rescue swimmer. In case…"

In case my corpse was floating downstream some-where.

"James Waterson the third, you ought to be ashamed of yourself. Don't even say things like that. Look at Becky's face. She's as white as a ghost."

"I am?" Rebecca was startled to be the topic of conversation when she'd been being good, which meant being silent.

Trey turned around in his seat to see her. "I'm sorry."

She shrugged, the good guest. "I was so busy being cold, drowning never crossed my mind."

Trey shot a look at his aunt. "I was thinking about cattle, not Rebecca."

Rebecca felt a smile tug at the corner of her mouth. "I feel another cow analogy coming on."

Trey briefly smiled at her.

She fell silent again, shy because she'd teased Trey in front of the two women.

He looked back out the window at the passing ranch land. "The cattle were herded into the gullies to get out of the wind. Now they gotta get driven right back out, before the water rises, or we'll be lassoing a bunch of heifers and hauling them out of the water. This time of year, they're heavy with calves. It'll be hard on the horses."

June started to laugh. "Oh, Trey, you're such a rancher. You're as bad as my father, always tyin' every lovin' thing back to his ranch."

Rebecca kept her gaze on his profile, devouring the sight of him when she couldn't touch him, although his expression was hard, his mouth tight.

"I'm sure Gus is on it," he said. "They're probably out there right now, driving them in this rain."

That sounded like some of the hardest, coldest, most miserable work Rebecca could imagine, yet Trey sounded almost wistful.

"Not you, Trey," Aunt June said, patting his knee after she turned on her blinker to turn into the James Hill. "You're going to eat some hot food and take a hot shower and get some sleep. You've already rescued your heifer for the day."

Rebecca liked his aunt's maternal tone, as sweetly bossy as anything she'd ever heard on a wholesome television show, but Emily slapped her palm into her forehead.

"Mom! You just called Becky a heifer."

The women chuckled, Rebecca being sure to chuckle politely, too, as the good guest who didn't take offense, but Trey said, "She goes by Rebecca."

His hard expression didn't change as they rattled over the cattle guard and headed to someone else's home.

Chapter Twelve

The house belonged to Patricia Cargill and Luke Waterson.

One look at the new master bedroom suite, and Rebecca knew whose elegance it reflected. This had to be Patricia's home.

"Gorgeous, isn't it?" Emily said. "My aunt and uncle—Luke's parents—were going to switch rooms with Luke when he got engaged. Since he lives here all the time, they were going to give him the master bedroom suite, and they were going to move into his bedroom. They're only here for roundup and Christmas and such, you know. But your sister, she insisted they keep the master, and she and Luke built this addition for themselves. That's one smart woman. I could live in here."

She's not really my sister, Rebecca almost said.

When someone has a good impression of you, for God's sake, don't correct them. Her mother had trained her too well. Letting people assume she was a Cargill was how Becky survived.

Rebecca didn't know any other way to get a free place to stay. Rebecca had no job, no money and only a few blue suitcases. Rebecca would have to continue being Becky for a while.

She showered under a rainfall spout, blew her hair dry at a vanity that reminded her of Dr Pepper and red lipstick, and then opened her suitcase to find clean clothes.

Christmas was only a few days away, but her mother had packed her for a tropical island vacation, if entertaining Hector Ferrique was a vacation. Rebecca craved holiday chic, a sultry red sweater and black leather boots, but those clothes hung in Patricia's closet. She didn't feel right, using a woman's things without her permission. All Becky had at her disposal were white capris and a pineapple print blouse that Audrey Hepburn would have looked girlishly adorable in.

She pulled ballerina flats gingerly over her once-frozen toes, and tip-toed into the kitchen, ready to eat politely and stay invisible, so that no one would remember that she should really be looking for her own place to live.

That's how it's done, Mother, I know.

Emily had thoughtfully plugged Rebecca's phone into a bedside radio that charged it, but Rebecca didn't turn it on, and she didn't check for messages. She already knew everything her mother had to tell her.

Trey was disappointed in Rebecca.

He hadn't known it was possible to think so highly of another person and yet be so disappointed. The Rebecca he thought so highly of, the Rebecca he would have loved for his aunt and uncle and cousin to meet, was hiding herself away.

They called her Becky all day, and she never corrected them. She smiled a lot and said practically nothing, a pretty mouse of a woman, easy on the eyes, for certain, but easily overlooked.

He was furious with her. Jamie had said she was in survival mode, but Trey knew there was no possible way her pulse was still one hundred and twenty. Hell, if she took a Valium to calm down, she'd be so sedate she might as well be that porcelain Christmas angel who never moved.

She'd gone to bed hours ago in the pristine new bedroom Luke had built for himself and Patricia. Aunt June and her husband were in his parents' master suite. Emily had taken Luke's old bedroom, which meant Trey was back after a ten-year absence in the same room he'd always known.

Company had obviously been using his bedroom over the past decade. His mother had converted it into a guest bedroom, taking down the Dallas Cowboys cheerleader posters and packing away the detritus of a teenage life. It was clean and masculine and comfortable, but she'd left the trophy shelf.

Trey lay on top of the navy bedding, warm enough in a pair of loose flannel pants to go without a shirt. With his hands tucked underneath his head and his feet crossed at the ankles, he glared at the shapes of those trophies in the dark. Potential was what they'd represented. Nothing more, no guarantees. That potential was no more.

But on the other side of the house, in a room built for a new marriage, lay a woman whose potential was limitless. She was young and smart and ready to break free from a bad situation, yet she was letting that potential go to waste. Since they'd returned to the house, she'd become a silent, decorative doll who wouldn't assert herself, not even to ask people to call her by the right name.

He was baffled. She had nothing to gain from hiding herself. Confusion fed his anger. The damned trophies fed his anger. The way his body ached for contact with Rebecca, the way his palms felt restless without her soft skin to soothe, fed his anger.

The door opened, and an angel in a long white robe stepped inside. She shut the door and leaned back against it, glaring at him in the moonlight.

"I can't sleep," Rebecca said, and it sounded like an accusation. "You put me in a room all by myself on the other side of the house."

She sounded as angry as he felt, and that fed his frustration, too.

"You're a big girl, Rebecca. You didn't like the arrangements? Then you should have said something."

"I'm a guest." She practically hissed the words at him. "Guests don't refuse to sleep in the bed they're offered. Was I supposed to tell your aunt that I wanted to shack up with you?"

She had a point, but the fact that she did hardly helped Trey's mood. "Did it occur to you to tell *me* you wanted to sleep with me? You've hardly said two words to me all evening."

"I'm a stranger here."

"Not to me. You could have talked to me." Their time was limited, and Trey was mad that they'd wasted the afternoon and evening, nearly a whole day, not talking. "You barely made eye contact with me all evening, but now that you can't sleep, you sneak in to see me."

"Oh!" Rebecca literally stamped her foot, whirled around and wrenched the door open. She was gone in a swirl of white fabric.

Trey wasn't sure he'd ever actually seen a woman mad enough to stamp her foot before. It had looked more adorable than fearsome on her, that perfect foot flashing through the fold of her robe, the foot that he'd warmed in his hands, the foot that might soon show signs of frostbite.

His anger dissolved. What an idiot he was. By the time they'd arrived at the house, he'd been rattled by the chaos of the hospital, embarrassed by his screwups, infuriated by yet another normal CT scan and a doctor's all-clear. He'd let his problems overshadow what mattered.

Rebecca mattered, yet he'd made her angry enough to stamp that fragile foot.

He headed after her, pulling on a T-shirt as he crossed the house. He was sure of where he was going, not only sure of where he was in the building, but sure that if Rebecca needed him, if she wanted him for any reason at all, he should be there for her. He burst into her room without knocking, catching her as she was about to turn off a bedside lamp by the four-poster bed.

She turned to see him and left the lamp on.

"I'm sorry," Trey said. "Again. I swear, Rebecca, I've never needed to apologize to anyone more often than you, which sucks, because you are the one woman that I never want to hurt. I'm sorry. If you want to sleep with me, I'm all yours."

"Isn't that magnanimous of you?" She lifted her chin at a haughty angle that would have fit the most regal queen. "I no longer require your services."

He looked at her, hard. "I think you do. I think you don't want to be cold, and you don't want to be alone, so we should sleep together, and that's final."

She raised one brow and tapped her foot, that fragile foot, in irritation.

Trey swallowed. "I'm not saying we have to have sex. We should share a bed to stay warm, because we're used to that now. We'd both sleep better."

After a long moment, she untied her robe's sash. "Fine, if that's the way you want it."

She dropped the robe to the floor, and Trey almost went to his knees. She was dressed in a version of a Christmas baby doll nightie, an X-rated version. The red puffed sleeves were exaggerated, the ruffle on the edge of the hip-length dress was green, but the dress itself was sheer. The tinsel that tied under her breasts hid nothing. The outfit had a cute and innocent silhouette but revealed everything that would make a man want the opposite. It worked. Too well.

"Where in the hell did you get that?" he demanded.

"It was in my suitcase."

"Take it off." It wasn't a sensual request, not a bedroom demand. It was an order, barked out in anger.

She frowned at him. "I thought you'd like it. It was meant to be an early Christmas present."

He drove his hand through his hair. "That's a fantasy outfit chosen by someone else to please a different man with different tastes. I never want to see it on you again."

For one second, she looked devastated at his words. Before he could curse himself and apologize to her, she started advancing on him, anger replacing dismay in her expression. She poked him in the shoulder.

"Listen. I've had a hard day. Make that two days. I've been scared out of my mind. I've been cold. I've been hungry. But the one bright spot has been you. I love being with you, but ever since we got to this house, you've been acting like you barely know me. Now you're mad at me for wearing something I know good and well looks sexy. If you don't want me anymore, Trey Waterson, just say so."

She'd never been more beautiful. This was sexy to him, this confidence, this will to challenge him.

"I want you," he growled. "I want you so bad it hurts, every minute."

"Then prove it." She pushed him down on the bed and clambered over him. Within seconds, they were tearing off tinsel and T-shirts, breathing hard, kissing harder.

Trey fought for clarity in the haze of desire. "Are you sure about this?"

"About what?" she asked, backing off him to yank down his pants, her expression one of fierce concentration.

"This is only your third time. You want...angry sex?"

She'd stripped him and was above him once more. She tossed her hair back. "Is there a law against it?"

Her sarcasm surprised him, but then Trey started to laugh, aware that he'd been conquered in every way by this virgin, this vixen, his Rebecca. She silenced him with her eager mouth, and their bodies took over, making demands and taking what they wanted from each other.

Afterward, in the quiet and the dark, with only starlight coming in through the picture window to light their bed, she sprawled on top of him and he smoothed her hair. He felt her eyelashes blink against his chest. She still wasn't sleeping.

"Close your eyes, sweetheart. I promise you, we'll still be here in the morning."

She sighed, and trailed her fingers down his arm. "Well, I'll be here, but you'll be back in your bed. We can't let your aunt June catch us. What would she think of me?"

She was still anxious to be thought of as a good little girl. It bothered Trey.

"I'm thirty-one years old. You're twenty-four. We've decided to be with each other. This is my house, and there's no way in hell I'm scurrying back to a guest room when I want to be with you. Aunt June will survive." He tried to lighten the mood. "She's had three kids and just as many husbands. I don't think she'll be shocked."

But Rebecca had gone very still. "Do you really own this house?"

There was something so grave in the way she asked, Trey knew it was not an idle question. "Yes, a third of it. A third of the ranch."

"Oh," she breathed, with a little catch in the sound. She raised her head and looked at him, doe eyes in the soft light. "Then could I stay awhile?"

He shouldn't have forgotten what she needed. She had nowhere to call home. She had no idea how long this temporary visit would last. He'd failed to give his lover security.

"Not because we had sex," she whispered, and he knew she was thinking of her mother. "I don't want that to have anything to do with it. I just need a place to stay."

He'd always had a home. Not his apartment in Oklahoma, but this ranch. He hadn't been back in ten years, it was true, but it had always been here, waiting, ready to welcome him if he needed it. That was a security that Rebecca had never known, not in her childhood, not as an adult. It was one he'd not appreciated before, but it was one he wouldn't take so lightly again.

"Rebecca Cargill, you have a place on the James Hill Ranch for as long as you want it. Whether you have sex with me or spit in my eye, you've got a roof over your head."

"I'm not really a Cargill," she whispered.

"I'm talking to you, Rebecca, not to a Cargill."

"I like the cow analogies better than spit in your eye." She wrinkled her nose and laughed a little bit, which he was glad to see. He wanted her to be happy.

Her laugh died away quickly. "I'd like to stay through

Christmas, and a little beyond. Just until I can figure out what to do next. I'll get a job. I won't impose on you forever."

She didn't intend to stay with him forever.

He'd worried about leading her on, knowing they'd be parting ways sooner rather than later. She'd said she loved him in the cabin, but he hadn't said it back, and she hadn't repeated it since. It ought to be a relief to hear her say that this time together was only an interlude for her, too.

Instead, it cut him to the quick.

"Close your eyes now, sweetheart. I'll be here in the morning."

But for how many mornings?

He'd never been the kind of man to wish for a miracle, but now he knew the miracle he'd choose: a forever of mornings.

Forever, with Rebecca Cargill.

Aunt June and her family left the next day to go to their own home for Christmas. June's other daughters would be there, bringing their own young families.

Trey left Rebecca cozied up on the couch in her tropical clothing, but with her feet wrapped in one of his mother's afghans. She had three days of newspapers to devour, something he thought might be more than a hobby to her. When she started sentences with "I read an article once," Trey knew that meant she'd read dozens of articles, every single day, as a teenager and adult. It had been her way to learn about the world her mother wouldn't let her join.

He left to check on the horses, an impulse that seemed to come naturally with being back at the ranch. It had been ten years, closer to eleven, so his favorites were gone, the horses sold to be pampered pets in their old age after a life of cowboy work. He chose a few of the current ranch horses that could carry a man his size and rode them briefly, get-acquainted rides in case he needed a horse while he was here.

The foreman, Gus, stopped by the paddock and gave him a terse update on the flooding. The river hadn't risen too far. The flood hadn't lasted too long.

"Luke will be glad to hear it," Trey said.

"You planning on riding out there to bring those ATVs back? 'Cause that horse in particular don't like the noise. She won't be real cooperative if you want her to follow you back while you're riding a machine."

"It'd be faster and easier to drive my truck out there. Most of it was easy terrain. I'll take two men and a can of gas, and they can drive the ATVs back." Trey remembered that although he was James Waterson at the James Hill Ranch, he was also new around here in a way. He owed Luke's foreman certain courtesies. "If you've got two men to spare, that is."

"Like I said, water went back down quick. Tomorrow's looking pretty light."

"All right, we'll do it then." Trey turned his horse from the fence, and took her around the pasture one more time.

It all felt so familiar. He felt so *normal*.

By the time he returned to the house, Rebecca had redecorated the fireplace. She'd taken down the wedding decoration and hung an evergreen garland with red bells and ornaments in its place. She asked him if it was okay to continue going through the decorations she'd found in the detached garage.

Trey thought it was a lot of trouble to decorate a house for just two people, but he knew it was her fantasy to have an old-fashioned Christmas, so he dragged as many boxes into the house as she wanted.

Rebecca had hung the wedding swag around the full-length oval mirror in the newlyweds' bedroom. As they stood before it, Rebecca taught him how to pronounce cheval glass, emphasis on the "-val," and Trey taught her how to enjoy it for their fourth round of sex, emphasis on the visual.

Their fourth time. Not that he was counting. Not that he was trying to commit every encounter to memory.

The fifth round was a challenge inspired by newspapers. During a dinner of leftover wedding hors d'oeuvres, Rebecca began the topic as she set her fork and knife precisely on the edge of her plate. "I read an article once that said the traditional missionary position is universally rated number one in polls about sexual habits."

Trey kept chewing. He even managed to swallow, with a chaser of sweet tea.

"But I wouldn't know about that," she continued conversationally, "because I'm always the one on top."

She put her elbow on the table and her chin in her hand, and sighed heavily, looking as wholesome as a daisy in her yellow-and-white beach dress. "Oh, you don't have to get up on my account. You've still got three more miniquiche on your plate."

"I read an article once," he said, as he tugged her behind him on the way to the bedroom, "that said well-read women make the best lovers."

"You can't believe everything you read in the papers."

He looked over his shoulder and winked at her. "Darlin', you've already proven that one is true."

For two more days, Trey enjoyed each round. He relaxed into a feeling of normalcy, and stopped trying to commit every moment to memory. He knew where he was. He knew everything about this ranch. It didn't seem possible that he could forget the new memories he was making now.

Trey did a little more ranch work, Rebecca did a lot more decorating, and they kept the sex lighthearted. Tomorrow would come. She'd find her job, and he'd return to Oklahoma, and there was no sense thinking about miracles like forever.

He'd already gotten the miracle of Rebecca. She'd survived an ice storm. She'd gifted him with her body. Even when Rebecca curled up next to him and made him watch movies about Christmas miracles, Trey knew better than to expect the universe to give him more than that.

Trey kept the right perspective for rounds eight and nine and ten, but it was Christmas Eve that did him in.

On the safety of the Navajo blanket, with the limestone fireplace warming them both, Rebecca was having her traditional Christmas. By the massive tree that she'd assembled from the box in the garage, she served him popcorn and hot chocolate as she hung the last ornament.

Her sweetness wasn't a matter of wardrobe, Trey already knew. Her confidence was real, too, and when mixed with her sweetness, the combination was like none other. Some of her ideas of daring adventures in bed were touching in their innocence. Tonight, she revealed a deck of cards and dared him to play blackjack for her idea of high stakes: every losing hand would require the loss of an article of clothing.

"Strip blackjack," she announced, as if she were a Roman emperor who'd just declared the start of a court-wide orgy.

Trey was so hopelessly charmed, so completely under her spell, that he agreed to the game before he remembered why he no longer played cards.

Rebecca dealt hearts and spades and clubs on the zigzag diamonds of the Navajo blanket.

Trey tried to focus on the numbers. The suites were not part of the game. He focused on the numbers seven and two in the corners of the cards, but some of the numbers were Js and Qs. They had a value, he knew, when added to two. Trey felt the sick feeling between his shoulder blades begin, while he prayed this Christmas was not about to go to hell.

Chapter Thirteen

"Hit me."

Rebecca pouted. "C'mon, Trey. It's no fun if you try to lose. The idea is for you to get me naked. You have to try to win, so that I have to take off a piece of clothing, not so that you have to."

It was as if the man had never played blackjack in his life. She'd even stopped a few hands ago to remind him of the rules. They needed to draw cards—take a hit—until their cards totaled as close to twenty-one without going over.

"You've got eighteen. Why would you want another card?"

She was watching his face closely, so she saw him blink as if he were surprised. Saw the way his mouth tightened. Saw him squint at the cards.

"Do you wear glasses?" she asked.

That question definitely surprised him. "There's nothing wrong with my eyes. Hit me."

"Fine." She dealt the next card off the top of the deck. A four. If he'd gotten a two or three, he would have beaten her. She smiled at him. "That was close."

"Hit me again."

She couldn't keep smiling.

"You already lost, Trey." She said it as kindly as she could, but her gentleness was lost on him as he glowered at the cards. Then he sat back and sent her a brilliant smile, too brilliant, and he pulled off his shirt.

"I know I lost. I needed to get rid of that shirt. It's too warm by the fire."

His bare chest was beautiful in the firelight. The lights were twinkling on the tree, and this Christmas Eve should have been her fantasy come true.

Instead, she felt cold.

"Trey, I think we should go to the hospital."

"Let me see your feet." He cupped her heel and slid off her sock, the warm wool one she'd borrowed from Patricia's drawer out of necessity. The soles of her feet were peeling from the frostbite, but there was nothing too awful to see, nothing black or green or dangerous.

"It's not my feet. It's you."

He kept his head down, her foot cradled in his hand.

"I read this article once, about the signs of stroke. It seems to me you're having an awfully hard time counting and remembering the rules. You're young for a stroke, but it's not impossible. I read this article—"

His head snapped up. "I don't need to go to the hospital."

She was startled at his anger; her foot jerked in his hand.

He set her foot down gently and gathered up the cards.

"You know what?" she said brightly, coming to her feet. She moved over to the sofa, with its end table and the old-fashioned, corded phone that had a permanent place on it. "You shouldn't be driving if we suspect an issue, and I'm not the world's best driver, so I'm just going to call an ambulance. That's the fastest way to get there."

He stood, as well. "Don't call 911."

She was tempted to obey him. He looked so normal, so smoothly coordinated, as he dragged his shirt back over his head. If she hadn't witnessed hand after hand of failed blackjack, she'd never believe there was anything wrong. But she had seen it, and it had scared her. She picked up the phone because she loved him, and she couldn't watch him suffer from an attack that could be silent but real.

He took the phone out of her hand and placed it back in its old-fashioned cradle. "I'm not having a stroke. I just hate to play cards."

It was a laughable statement, but he looked as serious as she felt, standing before the fireplace with his hands on his hips. He didn't touch her. He couldn't quite look at her as he said, "Hate is the wrong word. It's *can't*. I can't play cards."

The simple sentence cost him so much to say, he turned away from her to face the fire.

"You got the first few hands right, but then I think something happened. Did you feel anything? Sometimes people report they felt a pop or—"

"I can get things right sometimes, but then the harder I try, the harder it gets. It's stupid, but it's not a stroke."

"How long has it been like that?"

He braced on hand on the mantel and leaned closer to the fire. The flames lit him in golds and oranges.

"Forever," he said. "It feels like forever."

It was hard for her to imagine Trey being unable to do anything. He was invincible in her eyes, a man impervious to ice storms and unimpressed by hospitals. She'd been spying on him through the windows, watching him ride horses, awed by the way he could make them change directions or gallop or stop, anything at all he wanted. Every night, he handled her as easily, making her climax with a word in her ear and the press of his body, making her sleep with the warmth of his chest as he stroked her hair.

But he could not make cards add up to twenty-one.

She clasped her hands in front of herself, trying to sort through the implications. "It must be more than card games. Do you run into other things that are hard to do?"

"Now and then."

He didn't fool her with his stoic profile and his calm answers. She knew him, and she knew the tension in his shoulders was not right. Her curiosity was burning, but she wasn't going to ask him about things he did not want to talk about, not when he bore each question as if it were a turn of the screw.

"Okay, then." She held up her palms, and shrugged. *All done. No further questions.*

"I didn't mean to ruin your Christmas Eve." He didn't turn to her as he said it. He didn't see the smile she wanted him to see.

She dropped her hands. "It's supposed to be our Christmas Eve, not just mine."

He was so remote as he stared into that fire, alone with thoughts that caused him pain. *Look at me, I'm here. I want to help. I love you.*

But she couldn't say any of that. She'd told him she loved him once, in the cabin. She wasn't brave enough to whisper it again, not when he didn't feel the same. But he loved her touch. She could offer him that.

She walked to his side and placed her palm softly on his back, between his shoulder blades. The muscles were taut. She kept her hand there, waiting for the tension to release.

"If my idea of fun isn't your idea of fun, you could just say so next time," she said.

"It's not that easy."

She kissed his shoulder. "Actually, it is. 'Hey, sweetheart. I don't like to play cards. Let's do something else.' That would work."

Finally, finally, he pushed away from the mantel and turned toward her, and she slid her arms around his waist, fitting herself to him as she had from the first.

"This is still a great Christmas Eve," she said. "We've got the tree and the fire and the hot chocolate."

He gently ran his fingertips over her cheek, and returned her smile with a nearly authentic one of his own. "What other Christmas traditions are on your agenda? There's enough food in this house for a feast, but we're fresh out of plum pudding. We could go a-wassailing, but you'd have to tell me what that is, exactly."

She laughed, because he was trying to make her

laugh, and she loved him for it. "We should be nestled all snug in our beds with visions of sugarplums dancing in our heads."

"I like the bed part. I might take it as a challenge to drive those thoughts of sugarplums out of your head."

"Challenge accepted."

Their mood was only light on the surface, and as they bared themselves to one another, they stopped trying to be amusing. They kissed and touched and moved in silence. He was hurting inside, and she knew it.

Rebecca wrapped her whole self around him, telling him with her body what she could not say with her words. *I've got you. Hold on to me. You're not alone.*

It was what he'd given her when she'd been cold and hopeless.

She was afraid he still felt alone even after he reached his completion in her arms, so she pulled the covers over his shoulders and tucked herself tightly in with him, as if they shared the warm cocoon of a sleeping bag once more.

"You weren't supposed to get me anything for Christmas."

Rebecca said it at nearly the same time as Trey. They'd agreed to enjoy the holiday without shopping. Neither one of them had cared to leave the ranch in the days since they'd come back from the hospital.

Rebecca had another reason to avoid shopping. She hadn't wanted to use her credit card, because somehow, she seemed to be escaping her mother's attention.

It wouldn't last forever, but she wanted to delay the inevitable for as long as she could.

But here they were, sitting on the blanket under the tree on Christmas Day, holding gifts for each other. Rebecca was thrilled, because it gave her an excuse to be close to Trey. On the surface, everything seemed to be their usual smiles and friendship, but underneath, there was a distance between them that there hadn't been before.

He'd told her this morning that he needed to see to the horses, because he'd told the foreman to give everyone the day off. He'd told her this politely as he'd stood by the bed, already dressed. Then he'd left her there, alone.

Hours later, he'd returned, given her a quick kiss and headed for the shower. She'd asked him if he needed help soaping up. He'd smiled, but told her to stay and enjoy her newspapers, he'd join her in a minute.

Maybe she was being too sensitive. Maybe it was unrealistic to expect a man to be so into her, day after day. Maybe this distance was normal.

Normal or not, the distance hurt. The surprise Christmas gift helped. She let herself hope they would get back to the place they'd been.

"Open mine first," she said, cozying up to him in her white satin robe, wishing physical closeness could bridge the gap.

She'd made him a coupon booklet, although it had turned out less sleek and sophisticated than she'd pictured. She'd included coupons for the free use of mirrors and showers, one for each position they'd explored.

It had seemed very naughty and fun when she'd made it, but as he read it, she worried. He meant so much more to her than this.

The very last coupon said, "A hug and a kiss when you need it most." Not sex, but closeness. That was what she wanted for him, with him, for her.

He flipped through the book, that one-sided half-smile on his face. When he finished, to her great surprise, he raised the booklet to his lips and gave it a kiss.

"It's like a memory book," he said. "A chronicle of our time together. Every time I look at it, it will help me to—" He stopped himself. "I'll think of you."

Her heart stopped. Memories?

Their time was up. The distance he was putting between them made sense now. She closed her eyes and laid her head on his shoulder. "You must need to get back to your company in Oklahoma."

There was a long pause. She didn't lift her head or try to see his face. Her heart felt so heavy, she didn't want to try to read his expression or guess what he was thinking.

"Not yet," he said.

It was her reprieve. Her heart, pitiful thing that it was, wanted to cry with relief that for a little while longer, he would stay. She would enjoy his warmth, and store up memories, and hope they would keep the cold away after he left.

It would be like capturing sunshine in a jar, but she would try. She had to try.

She sat up, dry-eyed, and faced him with a smile. "So, do any of those coupons remind you of anything that looks like it would be particularly jolly on this Christmas Day?"

He ran his fingers along her jaw lightly, then pulled her in for a soft Christmas kiss.

"Open your gift," he said.

Inside the box was a letter. In black ink dashed on white paper, in wording so formal he could have copied it from a wedding invitation, Trey requested the honor of her presence at a genuine, traditional Christmas dinner, to be served at the River Mack Ranch.

"It's cheating," he confessed, "but when Mrs. Mac-Dowell called to invite us, I knew it was the best way to give you a traditional Christmas. You already know Jamie and his wife—ah, what was her name?"

"Kendry."

"Right. You already know them, so you won't be among strangers. Do you want to go? We don't have to, if you don't want to."

Did she want to spend time with him, among his friends, being a part of his life?

"I do."

Chapter Fourteen

Christmas at the River Mack Ranch made Rebecca happy, and that made it worth the effort for Trey. Nothing else would have induced him to accept the invitation. Social events were too fraught with ways for him to humiliate himself.

Yet, all the possibilities he'd braced himself to face for Rebecca's sake hadn't happened. The road between the James Hill and the River Mack was the same as it had been since his childhood. He hadn't needed to stop and think and check directions. He'd been able to get behind the wheel of his truck and drive his date to the MacDowells' house, like any man should be able to do.

Jamie's older brothers, Quinn and Braden, were closer to Trey's age, and he knew them better than he knew Jamie. They were here, instantly recognizable, part of the football memories that had been so recently unlocked. If anything, it was Quinn and Rebecca who seemed to have a memory problem. They spent a minute saying how familiar each looked, until they recalled meeting when Rebecca had last visited Patricia. Quinn and Patricia were both with Texas Rescue, that much Trey absorbed.

He turned to greet Mrs. MacDowell. She looked exactly as Trey remembered her. Since he'd so recently survived Aunt June's hugging and fussing, Mrs. MacDowell's was less alarming.

Trey managed not to blurt any random thoughts, taking a moment before speaking to be sure what he said was appropriate. At dinner, however, with the food and confusion and conversation, it happened. As he watched everyone devouring turkey and gravy, he said, "Rebecca devours newspapers."

The awkwardness passed quickly. The beat of surprise from the MacDowells at his end of the table quickly turned into more conversation about the local newspapers and their coverage of the hospital when its CEO had been arrested for embezzling.

Braden was the new CEO. As the meal went on and information and updates from a decade's absence rolled in, Trey could feel his brain shutting off. He fought it. For Rebecca, he wouldn't withdraw and turn into a silent, sullen guest.

But he could only concentrate on so many things at once. He stopped eating in order to focus on the faces around him. Half the people were familiar, which saved him, because there were also strangers. There was a baby, a newborn who slept while everyone sang her praises, and a toddler who fed himself mashed potatoes with two chubby hands. Not only was Jamie married to what-was-her-name with the ponytail, but Braden was married, as well. Quinn was engaged. Those women were all here, easy enough to talk with since Trey didn't really need to remember who went with which brother or which baby belonged to whom. They were all MacDowells. That was all he needed to know.

No math of any kind came up in conversation, so all in all, Trey felt he'd managed to pull off a decent Christmas for Rebecca.

But he was exhausted, as if he'd taken final exams at school, math and history and literature, one after the other without a break. That kind of tired.

After dinner, the men pulled him into their father's old den, because there was a college bowl game on television. It was time for football. Trey dropped into the nearest armchair, too exhausted to drink the beer that Quinn pressed into his hand.

On television, a player got clobbered, the kind of hit that made everyone wince in sympathy—except Trey. He paid no attention, relieved to be sitting still and letting his mind take a break.

"You took a hit like that, senior year, against Anderson High," Braden said to Quinn.

"That was nothing compared to the one Trey took against Killeen." Quinn tapped his beer can to Trey's. "Remember that one? I think it was the only time coach let you sit out one whole play before putting you back in."

The MacDowells made all the appropriate manly noises, everyone remembering their tough coach, and glory days.

"You remember that?" Quinn asked him again.

Trey forced himself to pay attention. "A game against Killeen?"

"Yeah, senior year. Went into overtime. C'mon, you

remember. You won it with a forty-yard pass to that freshman, the cocky kid, what's his name?"

"Zach Bishop." Trey wanted to say he'd just seen him recently, in the helicopter after the ice storm, but putting together all the right words to tell the story would take too much effort.

"That's the one," Jamie agreed.

Still, Trey felt better. He'd remembered a name everyone else had forgotten. He was too hard on himself, maybe, when he spoke of someone like Jamie's wife as what's-her-name. Quinn, who was a doctor, had just done it himself.

"It was Bishop who got your brother to volunteer with the fire department," Quinn said. "They're working together for Texas Rescue now."

"No, my brother's on his honeymoon."

All three MacDowells looked at him instead of the television. Trey knew he'd said something off. He gripped the cold beer can.

"You remember that game against Killeen?" Jamie asked again, sounding more like a serious doctor than a kid brother. Either was trouble Trey didn't want.

"Not really." Trey kept his gaze on the television. They were strapping the player to a backboard, immobilizing his neck with a foam brace.

Jamie nodded at the screen and spoke to the group at large. "We don't let them back in the game anymore. They've gotta sit out at least a week of practice, and then they have to see me or their own family doctor for clearance. Coach is pretty pissed at the team doctor for enforcing the new rules."

"Let me guess," Trey said, taking a moment to be sure he was about to say something normal. "The new team doc is named MacDowell. Jamie?"

"Yep. Coach says he's in the business of winning championships. I'm in the business of preventing brain injuries. He thinks my first season as team doctor should be the last, but I told him that wasn't his call to make."

Quinn and Braden exchanged a look, brothers ready to defend their own, but Jamie laughed, breaking the tension in the room. "It's pretty satisfying to see the old man's face when I pull rank on him."

"Well, my wife's gonna pull rank on me if I hide out here much longer." Braden left first, but they all returned to the main part of the house, Trey hauling himself out of the armchair last.

The women were cooing over the babies, and before Trey's eyes, the men started cooing over the women. That's how it looked to him. Each man had a woman who smiled when he walked up to her, someone pretty in her Christmas finery to lift her face and accept a kiss on the cheek or lips.

Then Braden picked up his newborn child. Braden, older than them all in school, the first to make varsity, the first to graduate, the one they'd all looked up to, *that* Braden looked at that baby, and that baby looked at him, and Trey could've seen the love a mile away. Braden was a goner for a baby girl who fit in the palms of his hands, head over heels with no turning back.

I want that.

Trey would never have it, because no one had ever

strapped him to a backboard and cradled his neck in foam.

On Christmas Day, in his neighbor's living room, James Waterson III knew, finally, what was wrong with him. It wasn't that he was lazy. It wasn't that he didn't try hard enough. He was not stupid, and he was not insane.

He had brain damage.

The doctors had said he didn't. The tests had all been normal. Ten years ago, they'd been wrong.

Millions of players had come through just fine—his own brother had played football without incident—but not Trey. He'd taken that hit, the dangerous kind, and he'd taken it more than once. More than twice. He'd been praised for his toughness and his ability to perform when his ears were ringing and his vision was blurred.

He stood in the doorway, watched the holiday scene before him and finally understood.

Then his worst nightmare came true. A young woman came in from the kitchen, cute with brown bangs yet sexy in a red sweater, and Trey thought, *Damn, she's pretty. Who is that?* Then recognition exploded in his mind, and he knew Rebecca and everything about her.

But for one millisecond, he'd lost his memory of her.

He wouldn't allow it. Nothing else mattered, not the strangers or the friends. Not the noise and the food. The women's laughter, the babies' tears—he cared for none of it. If his brain could only think of one thing at a time, then all of that had to go, because the only thing he absolutely had to be able to hold on to was Rebecca.

"We've got to leave now." He grabbed her hand and started pulling her to the door.

"Trey!" She hissed his name quietly, and tugged on his hand.

He stopped, because she wanted him to stop. She slipped her hand from his, went to pick up her purse and kissed Jamie's wife on the cheek. She thanked everyone and wished them a merry Christmas, and made a proper exit out of his botched one. Everyone smiled at them as they left.

Trey drove straight home. When Rebecca asked what the problem was, he couldn't explain.

He left the light on in the bedroom, and made love to her while holding her face in his hands. He made her look at him, so he could see her eyes and remember their exact shade of brown. With every stroke, he committed her to his memory. With every roll of his hips, he tried to make her a permanent part of him. He would not lose her. He couldn't bear to lose her, and he told her so. With his body and with his words.

He felt clumsy, his brain so tired from the holiday, and he didn't know if he was saying the right thing.

"You. It's you. You're everything."

Afterward, as she sprawled on his chest and he stroked her hair, she said, "I love you."

He was afraid to close his eyes and go to sleep, because if she wasn't there when he woke, he would die.

Chapter Fifteen

Trey stabbed the pitchfork into the hay. His brain was still tired from yesterday's dinner at the MacDowells', but his body was not. Physically, he felt strong and rested, so he'd left Rebecca in the four-poster bed and come to the barn to work off some energy. The cowboys he'd encountered—his own damned ranch hands, technically—had found work elsewhere on the ranch.

Trey forked more hay into the stall of an unappreciative horse. The mare picked up on his frustration and showed her disapproved by shaking her mane and blowing air through her soft nose.

"What are you doing, Waterson?" he muttered under his breath. He stopped and leaned on the pitchfork.

He was screwing everything up, that's what he was doing. Last night, tired and emotional, he'd crossed the line from an *interlude*, a pleasant week or two with the lovely Rebecca Cargill, and taken it to a different level.

Sex like they'd had last night wasn't just sex. It was the basis for a different kind of relationship. It was like laying a cornerstone to start a foundation for something big. It was dangerous, because it would make Rebecca think that the cornerstone had been laid for a reason, that it would support something built to last.

It wouldn't. It was just a brick, not a building. Their relationship was going nowhere.

"Brain damage." It made him sick to his stomach to say the words out loud, so he forced himself to say them, to get used to the feel of them on his tongue. He stabbed the hay again. "Brain damage."

Just because those freakish faults had a name and a cause didn't make them go away. He understood now why he'd let down every person who'd thought he had potential. The knowledge changed nothing. He was still the man who forgot to put water in the coffeepot and who got lost driving to client sites.

He was going back to Oklahoma, to run his landscaping business in his own brain-damaged way and to enjoy the occasional company of women who didn't want to get too serious. In the meantime, he needed to keep the proper perspective with Rebecca. They had a great time in bed. Their physical chemistry worked for them, for fun and friendship. He'd help her get set up in her first job and first apartment, and they'd part as friends, better for having known one another.

There'd been no Christmas miracle. Nothing had changed.

A piercing wolf whistle split the air in the barn. The horses shied and whinnied. Trey put a calming hand on the nose of the mare next to him and turned to see Rebecca, of course, standing with both hands over her mouth and her eyes wide with alarm.

"I'm so sorry," she said. "I didn't think about the horses. You just look sexy with a pitchfork."

It was too damned hard not to smile at Rebecca. Trey let himself grin as he nodded toward the aisle. The horses had gone back to their oats, only a few stamping a hoof to let them know how they felt about the interruption. "They're fine. They'd appreciate it if you didn't do that too often."

She came up to him, her pink parka unzipped to reveal a tropical blouse, her slacks formfitting. The parka and slacks were her clothes from the cabin, retrieved with the ATVs, washed and fresh now, but they reminded him how close he'd come to losing her once before.

Keep it light. Friendship. Chemistry. An interlude.

"Are we all alone in here?" Rebecca asked, running a finger along a stall door, pretending it was an idle question.

Trey kissed her lightly, a good-morning kiss. She smelled fantastic. She looked fantastic, with her hair brushed loose and her face clean and natural. "Just you, me and the horses."

"Have you ever had sex in a stable?"

His body tightened in response. He wanted her too much. He couldn't have casual sex with her. Not yet. Not this morning.

He turned away, and lifted another forkful of hay. "Having sex with your boots on is disrespectful to a woman. You don't take your boots off in a barn."

"But have you ever had sex in a barn? This barn?"

Trey's brain might not work well, but he knew better than to tell a woman about experiences with another woman.

"I wouldn't sleep with someone I didn't respect."

"I'm not talking about sleeping."

He rolled his eyes at that, but found he was grinning as he spread more hay.

Rebecca stood on her toes to look into the stall of a dappled gray mare. He was glad to see her feet caused her no pain. The frostbite was nearly healed.

Keep it light.

"If people have sex near them, do the horses whinny or kick the stalls or get mad?" she asked.

"The horses don't care."

"A-ha! You have had sex in a barn."

He didn't know whether to laugh or cry at her persistence. He stabbed the pitchfork into a tightly tied bale and left it there, upright, before he turned to face her. "No, I have not had sex in this barn. I've had my-father-would-kill-me-if-I-got-a-girl-pregnant-so-we're-sure-gonna-fool-around-but-not-go-all-the-way in this barn."

They stared each other down. He refused to admit he hadn't quite intended to say that.

"Wow," she said, first one to blink. "That sounds like it was kind of fabulous to be a teenager. Was it wonderful, growing up here?"

The expression on her face was so full of yearning, Trey looked up to the rafters to guard his heart. He could imagine her unstable childhood, stepparents and siblings and homes changing too often. As she'd become a teenager, he doubted she'd had the chance to taste love with a boy her age. Hell, she hadn't been allowed to choose her own clothes. Her mother had stolen her childhood.

Trey had lived a great life, the best of childhoods, until he'd become an adult.

He looked at Rebecca again. "Yes, I was lucky to grow up here. I'm sorry you never got to fool around in a barn."

He didn't voice the rest of his thought. *We're opposites, me with my great childhood and lousy adulthood. You had a bad childhood, but your adult life will be beautiful.*

Rebecca didn't seem to be thinking anything quite so philosophical. She'd advanced on him slowly, a woman walking in a way that was anything but childish.

She slid a finger between the pearl-button snaps of his plaid shirt. "Just how sorry are you about my lack of barn experience?"

"I can't help you with the not-go-all-the-way part." He slid his hands down the curve of her backside, then scooped her off her feet with his hands under her thighs. She wrapped her legs around his waist naturally as he pressed her against the door to a stall. That particular horse, at least, minded a little bit, and moved away from them.

Rebecca kept toying with his shirt. "I'm a little worried about this being your first time. If you've never had sex in a barn before, are you going to be able to figure out how to do it with your boots on?"

"I've got some ideas. What happens if they work?"

"I'll make you a coupon, so you can do it again."

Trey watched Rebecca as she made her way back to the house. His body felt better than ever. His mind was still screwed up.

What the hell are you doing, Waterson?

Rebecca looked considerably more rumpled leaving than she had when she'd come in, but she walked with a bounce in her step, peeking back at Trey now and then with a look on her face like she was the cat that had eaten the canary.

Trey grinned back at her. She should look like that; she'd gotten her way.

He leaned against the barn's door frame, hands in his pockets when they should have been on the pitchfork, keeping an eye on her for the pleasure of it. He had to shake his head at himself and their foolishness. Anyone on the ranch could've taken a look at the two of them and known what was up.

Just keeping it light. Friendly-like, until I get back to Oklahoma.

He needed to get back to work. Not to the pitchfork, but to his real job. Winter was the slow season for a landscaper, of course, so it had been fine to leave his lead crew with the truck keys and orders to handle the basic routine. But Trey was the owner, and an owner couldn't leave a business and expect it to run itself.

Not the way this ranch got by without him. Luke had done well. Trey knew Luke hadn't had much of a choice, because Trey had pretty much skipped town and their parents had decided to retire young, but the James Hill Ranch was thriving in Luke's hands.

Rebecca disappeared into the house. Into her home, the only home she had right now. His grin faded. Trey was giving her a place to live, but he was being careful to give her nothing else. Sex in the stables had been fun. A little playtime. Nothing more.

He'd messed that up last night, making love to her with such intensity. They were back on track now. Light and breezy, not building any kind of foundation.

Trey turned back into the barn. He couldn't think, standing still. That wasn't part of any brain injury. He'd always done his best thinking while doing something physical. What he needed right now was something to throw. Hurling a football would clear his thoughts, but there wasn't one in sight, and no one around to catch it if there were.

He grabbed a lasso off the wall, and headed through the barn to go out the far side. Coils in his left hand, loop in his right, he walked toward the paddock and started swinging the loop. He built up the motion, keeping the circle slow, turning his wrist with the loop, feeling muscles move in a way they hadn't for ten years. With the rope at its apex, he let go, not throwing so much as guiding its trajectory, the way he'd been doing it since middle school.

He missed.

The rope bounced off the paddock's fence post and hit the dirt.

Trey pulled it back toward himself, coiling it again. He needed to be able to do this. If he couldn't throw a decent lasso, he couldn't stay on the ranch. Regardless of how right it felt to be here, and despite the fact that it was the one place on earth he didn't feel disoriented, Trey would not stay if he could not do the work. He wouldn't be able to survive the sympathy if he was treated as the poor kid who'd gotten hit in the head. He'd rather mow lawns in Oklahoma than have his own ranch hands pity him.

He built the lasso's momentum, and let it go. It landed around the fence post. Reflexively, Trey pulled it taut. Then he fed it some slack and flicked his wrist to jump the lasso off the fence post.

He gathered it back in, and threw it again.

The fence post was too easy. Trey transferred a few coils into his loop hand, enough to gain an extra ten feet or so, swung the circle over his head and let it sail to a farther post.

He snagged that post and pulled the loop taut, all reflex. This time, the post was too far away for him to flick the rope off. He walked toward it, winding up the rope as he went, thinking about what he needed to think about: Rebecca.

What the hell are you doing, Waterson?

He was laying a foundation with her, that was what he was doing. It wasn't just built out of the serious lovemaking, the kind they'd shared last night or her first time, *their* first time, in the cabin. It was all of it. Every blush in the mirror, every slippery encounter in a soapy shower. Each time they were together, they set another brick in the foundation.

He could tell himself this morning in the stables had

been just for fun, but it had added to that foundation. When he hauled in a box of decorations or she handed him a section of the newspaper, they built something solid. Every stomp of her foot, every marshmallow in the cocoa, it all counted. All of it.

Closer now to the fence post, Trey flipped the lasso free. The foreman was walking toward him from the direction of the cattle sheds. They met at the paddock's fence.

"Been a while, huh?" Gus's voice matched his look. Tough, weathered, cowboy to the core.

Trey nodded, once. "I'll take that to mean it looks as rusty as it feels."

Gus turned and spit some tobacco juice, a nasty habit that Trey had been dying to try when he was eleven. Gus had let him. Trey had turned green and manfully announced he would be a tobacco-free cowboy. That had been before he'd decided to be an NFL quarterback. He'd ended up being neither.

"Son, your rusty is still better'n most boys' best."

Trey raised an eyebrow at that. Those were high words of praise from the foreman.

"How's landscaping treating you?"

"It's a living." Trey was mildly surprised at the personal question. It looked like Gus wanted to have a chat.

Trey rested his arm on the post and squinted against the Texas sun, bright even in winter, as he gazed across the paddock to the pasture beyond. That pasture, not too far away, was hardly ever used, because grass didn't like to grow there.

It was a landscaping nightmare, an acre or two of tough soil on a bit of a rise, but Trey knew what would grow there: olive trees. The agricultural magazines he read as part of his profession had been featuring olive oil and wine presses in Texas Hill Country for a couple of years now. Trey didn't know squat about grapevines, but trees were a different matter.

That pasture had always been underused. He should plant a couple of acres of olive trees there, sell the fruit to one of the local presses and turn a little profit on land that served no purpose.

If he were here to oversee it, that was. His brother didn't know trees. Trey couldn't plant an orchard and leave it for another ten years.

"Been meaning to ask you, son," Gus began, and Trey knew the reason Gus had sought him out was about to become clear, "about that new hand Luke wants hired. I've got someone in mind."

Luke and Trey and their father had held a three-way conference call last month. Luke had asked them to sink some of the year's profits into hiring more ranch hands.

Trey remembered the conversation clearly now, because the memories came easier out here on the land with a lasso in his hands. He remembered the guilt he'd felt, the guilt he always felt about the ranch he mostly ignored.

Luke and his new wife intended to make the ranch house their home, but she was the director of Texas Rescue and Relief, the same organization that had sent the helicopter, and her office was in downtown Austin. They planned to keep her high-rise apartment, and spend time there, as well.

I'm not expecting my wife to commute from the ranch all the way to downtown Monday through Friday, and I'm not expecting to live apart from my bride most days, either.

They'd agreed to his plan, but Trey had known it had been more of an ultimatum. Luke was done with being tied to the ranch three hundred and sixty-five days a year. If neither Trey nor their father were willing to shoulder some of the responsibility, then they'd better hire someone to do it for them.

Now Gus was asking Trey about one of those new hires. Trey was the wrong man to ask. He'd just come to the ranch for the wedding.

"Has Luke met him?"

"No." Gus spit again. "Luke's gone a month. This boy needs a job now, so I figured you could give the okay."

Trey tied off the rope into a knot every cowboy knew, an action he hadn't done since he was nineteen, but it came naturally, anyway. "We trust your judgment, Gus. You don't need a Waterson's permission to hire a ranch hand for the James Hill. You know that."

"Well, yeah, but this'n is different. He's my nephew, so I don't want it looking like I'm giving salaries to my own family. Good boy, but can't seem to stick with a job in the city. I thought the ranch might be better for him."

This was a delicate subject. Gus wouldn't want to

say someone in his family was a failure, but not being able to hold down a job was a red flag in Trey's book.

"Does he know cattle?"

"Nope."

"Horses?"

"Nope."

Trey hung the coiled rope on the fence post, letting his silence speak for itself. Gus knew better. Maybe he'd asked so that he could go back to his nephew and honestly say he'd tried.

"But he's strong. A Marine. Did his time overseas. He knows how to get up before the roosters tell him to and how to put in a full day. That's more than you can say for half these wanna-be cowboys."

Trey rubbed his jaw. So that was the rest of the story. A war veteran, having a hard time adjusting to civilian life. He put his boot on the bottom rung of the fence. "A three-month contract, then. We can always use someone with a strong back. We'll see if he likes the ranch and if the ranch likes him. That's three months to learn enough horses and cattle to make himself useful. If it works out, we can add him to the roster for roundup this spring."

Gus tugged on the brim of his cowboy hat. "That's a fair deal. Thank you."

As Gus walked away, Trey studied the dead land of the not-too-distant pasture. He could bring it back to life with a nice olive grove.

Hell, the view from over there was pretty nice. A house could sit in the middle of the grove, nothing fancy, just a straightforward, square limestone. Big porch, to take advantage of the view. Modern inside, the kind of layout where the kitchen and the living room were one big space. Rebecca would like that. She could decorate the hell out of it at Christmas, hang little twinkly lights on the porch and stuff. He'd see them when he rode his horse back after a day on the range.

God, his chest hurt at the picture of it.

He stacked his fists on top of the fence post and rested his forehead on them, almost a prayerful position. What if...what if the next time Luke asked Trey to run the ranch with him, Trey dumped the guilt and said yes?

He felt like he could do it. He didn't get lost out here. He could lasso and ride. Making decisions for the ranch like the one Gus had just asked him to make came easily, the same kind of decisions he'd been making for years for his business in Oklahoma.

The specter of his last roundup loomed large in the wreckage of his memory. He could brand a cow upside down again, or do something else that made him look like a drunken fool. But he was thirty-one years old now. He didn't care to tell anyone about his brain injury, but if he said something stupid the way he had in the hospital when he'd thought Aunt June needed a ride home in his truck, could he just let it slide and carry on?

And Rebecca...

Trey lifted his head again and looked at his dead pasture. Would a small house in a big olive grove be enough? Would it make up for the fact that she'd have a husband who couldn't help his kids with their ele-

mentary school homework? A husband who could forget which order to put the clothes in the washer and
dryer? The shame of it made him not want to even try.

But Rebecca...

If he truly loved her, he'd let her find a better man,
one without a bad brain. The idea of cutting her loose
to build a life with another man caused a pain that felt
like rage inside him.

He couldn't let her go. He'd found her, he'd warmed
her back to life with his own body, and they'd started
laying a foundation together, brick by brick.

He was going to keep her.

If she'd have him.

He started walking back toward the ranch house
to find out.

Chapter Sixteen

Rebecca sat in the mudroom and pulled off her boots. They were pink and designer-name and expensive, but they hadn't kept her feet warm during an ice storm. When she got her first paycheck, she was going to buy new ones. Better ones.

She hung up her ski parka. That, at least, had been as functional as it was fashionable. Her mother had accidentally outfitted her in something useful despite its childish shade of pink. Since the coat was warm, Rebecca couldn't really justify buying a new one right away, but she would, someday. Maybe something more ranch-like, natural leather with a sheepskin lining, like Trey wore. Hers would be nipped in a bit at the waist, more feminine in style.

Sorry, Mother, no more shapeless clothes to hide my figure. You're just going to have to admit you're old enough to have a grown-up daughter.

She walked through the black-and-white kitchen and into the comfy family room, where she'd decked the halls to her heart's content. There, standing by the ornament-laden Christmas tree, was her mother.

"Hello, Becky. Merry Christmas, baby girl, one day late."

It wasn't possible. Rebecca had accidentally, horribly conjured her by thinking of her in the mudroom.

Her mother had chosen the perfect place to stand. Morning sunlight came in the window behind her, making a halo effect around the edges of her dark hair, sparkling off the silver threads in her loose black blouse. Her mother hit just the right casual note by wearing it tucked into flattering black jeans. She looked, as always, fabulous.

"Come here, Becky. I've surprised you terribly, haven't I? No one answered the knock, but I knew an old-fashioned ranch like this would have the door open to visitors." Her mother laughed and held out both hands, simply delighted to see her.

Rebecca, who had been obedient for twenty-four years, automatically responded and crossed the room toward her mother. They were obviously on stage. She looked to see who the performance was for. A man in a plain navy suit stood by the front door, but his suit wasn't cut well enough to make him important. As she rounded the sofa, she saw, sitting in the winged-back armchair, the man for whom her mother was being so charming. Hector Ferrique, in crushingly expensive casual clothing, smiled at her.

Her mother took her hands and kissed her on each cheek. "How was Patricia's wedding? Did my ex-husband perform his duties adequately?" She sent a mocking look Hector's way with that comment, to let him know that she'd found the infamous Daddy Cargill's performance not up to her standards—unlike her dear Hector, no doubt.

"I didn't get to see Daddy," Rebecca murmured, obedient and vague, as she knew she should be.

Even as she followed her mother's cues, her mind raced. She could see things differently now. Surely, her mother had been sleeping with Hector in Rebecca's absence. Little Becky had flown away, and her mother must have gone to the Caribbean and done some explaining—and some apologizing. Some substituting.

Your mother is a call girl? Trey had asked Rebecca in the cabin, trying to understand her life.

Rebecca freed her hands from her mother's grasp and clasped them before herself. Her mother was not a call girl, but she had used sex or the promise of sex to keep a roof over their heads and to pay for Becky's private primary education. Rebecca found that sad and almost humbling. She ought to be grateful, but her mother had never acted like it had been a sacrifice, only a triumph.

The part of her that was still little Becky couldn't find it in herself to feel thankful for her mother's triumphs. For the past six years, because of her mother's need to keep men sexually attracted to herself, Becky had been deprived of a college education and a normal transition to adulthood. It was a sick thing, to keep another person eternally at age eighteen.

Rebecca had made that transition to adulthood now. Survival in an ice storm had a way of changing a person. Trey had never known her as Becky. Being treated by him like she was a whole and independent person affected how she saw herself.

"Your mother explained about your scheduling conflict." Hector spoke from the armchair like it was his throne. "I was very disappointed not to have your company this holiday."

Trey!

But Trey had stayed at the stables. He had things to do on the ranch. If he'd taken one of the horses out, he might not be back for hours. Rebecca was on her own.

She turned her back on Hector, unwilling to engage in even the most mundane conversation with a man who only wanted her because she looked like she was underage.

She was afraid she still looked that way. Her slacks were too long without her boots on. It was hard to look sophisticated in socks. But she was no child. She'd just seduced a cowboy. The man of her choice, handsome and strong, had been unable to resist her.

She unclasped her hands and stopped waiting for her mother's next move. "What do you need from me, Mother?"

"Need from you? Don't be silly, sweetie. I came to take you back home now that the wedding is over. Hector and I enjoyed Bimini but without you…well, it just wasn't the same. Your sister must still be on her honeymoon, so there's no reason for you to stay here. Patricia is gone, isn't she?"

Her mother was scared of Patricia Cargill. Rebecca had known that, even as a child. It was, after all, why she'd come to the James Hill Ranch: to hide behind Patricia's wedding gown skirts.

Rebecca felt Hector's gaze on her, and she hid behind those skirts again. "Patricia's out at the moment. I'm not sure when she'll return."

Her mother narrowed her eyes. "She's out?"

"Yes." Rebecca raised her chin and met her glare.

"Hmm…" Her mother moved from her picturesque spot by the tree and began strolling through the room, gliding her hand along the fireplace mantel, above the Christmas garland Rebecca had hung. Her gaze moved about the room, judging, weighing, evaluating. She paused at the far end of the mantel. "The fireplace is unique, very Texas. I'm sure Patricia will keep it when she remodels. The exposed roof beams have a rustic appeal."

She left the fireplace to sit on the arm of Hector's chair, a route that required her to pass Rebecca. As she brushed by Rebecca, she hissed in her ear. "She's on her honeymoon. Don't be an idiot."

Her mother perched on the armrest, forcing Rebecca to turn back around and face Hector, *Mr. Ferrique*, as her mother continued talking. "Patricia will keep those features, I'm sure. She's always had a good eye. The rest will have to be gutted. You're saying that's where she is? At the designer's? Well, if she's not back by the time you're packed, you'll just have to leave your sister a note. Hector's plane can't be kept waiting forever. Go pack, sweetie."

"No, thank you." Rebecca felt the significance of her stiff words. Her heart pounded, but the weight of the world seemed to lift from her shoulders. Three little words had never been so liberating. "I've decided to live here. I won't be returning to Boston. I was going to send for my things."

That had been a tactical error. From the way her mother's eyes narrowed, Rebecca knew she should have called the staff at the Cape Cod home and had them ship her belongings the day Trey had told her she could stay. She'd never get her things now. Not one thing.

It's okay. I'm going to have a job. I'll buy my own things.

In the meantime, she wouldn't starve and she wouldn't freeze, because Trey would support her.

Just as Hector supported her mother.

Something inside her protested that it wasn't the same thing, but as she looked at her mother perched beside her provider, she knew the truth. Had Trey been in the room, Rebecca would have sat with him. He provided all her material needs, and she…seduced him. Kept him happy.

She was just like her mother.

Hector pulled back the cuff of his sweater with a neat jerk and made a show of checking the time on his Rolex. Then he rested his hand on her mother's thigh, and drummed his fingers impatiently. Just once.

Her mother got the message. With a quickness of mind that had always impressed Rebecca, she changed tactics.

"I should have guessed that once a Cargill returned to Texas soil, she wouldn't want to leave. There's nothing more Texan than an oil baron's daughter, is there?" She laughed her martini and diamonds laugh, letting it taper off into a sigh. "It looks like I've got a little family matter to address. We won't bore you, Hector."

Her mother stood and threaded her arm through Rebecca's. "Let's take this to the kitchen, Becky. Show me where they keep the coffee."

Rebecca had never been a match for her mother. She'd learned not to disagree so long ago, she couldn't recall ever telling her mother no. Her mother never argued with her, for Rebecca never opposed her. But she was disagreeing with Mother today, and the resulting battle was worse than she could have imagined.

Back in the cabin, Trey had said she'd been trying to break out of prison. The analogy had resonated with her. She'd always known the prison guard would be harsh if she were caught. The actual sting of the guard's baton, however, could not have been prepared for. Each verbal hit was painful, even though she'd known it was coming.

"You stupid child. Patricia Cargill got here first. There is no room for you. You would have known better, if you had half a brain in your head."

They were sitting at the kitchen table, steaming mugs in front of them. Appearances were preserved. Anyone walking in would see a mother and daughter catching up over coffee. Her mother delivered all her blows quietly, hissing her words through perfectly white teeth.

"Damn it, Becky, use your head. This is your chance.

You can have everything. The house on Cape Cod. Trips around the world. You'll be able to point at anything in any store window, and it will be yours."

"I don't want that," she said quietly. Respectfully.

Her mother slapped her palm on the table, making Becky jump as the sugar bowl rattled. "You don't know what you're saying. Patricia will not want you underfoot in this house. You're younger than she is. Men are drawn to innocence. You think she's going to want her husband looking at you breakfast, lunch and dinner?"

"I'm going to get a job and move out soon."

"Oh, please." Her mother closed her eyes as if Becky's ignorance caused her pain. "This is what we're going to do. We'll return to Boston with Hector. If you've taken it into your head that you can do better, then we'll start looking. Cape Cod is too small. We'll stay in town and let you be seen at some clubs, so people will realize you're twenty-one. You'll need a new wardrobe. Nothing too dramatically different, at first."

"No." Rebecca stood up. "I don't want to start clubbing in Boston, Mother. I'm twenty-four, and I'm staying here."

The sound of the mudroom door opening made her knees go weak with relief. She turned to see Trey coming in as always, stomping the dirt from his boots, unfastening his coat. "Trey?" she said, trying to sound calm.

He looked up immediately. She must not have sounded very calm, because he came directly into the kitchen with his coat and boots on. After the briefest of glances at her mother, his attention was all for her. "Are you all right?"

He stood next to her, very close, and placed his hand in the small of her back as he removed his hat.

Her mother sat up very straight, missing nothing.

Rebecca took a deep breath. "Mother, I'd like you to meet Trey Waterson. Trey, this is my mother, Charlene Lexington Maynard."

Trey calmly tossed his hat on the table. It knocked her mother's coffee spoon sideways. He nodded, once. "Ma'am."

"Oh, call me Charlene, please."

Her mother was all gracious smiles, but Rebecca could see the wheels in her mind turning. She'd counted on Patricia and her husband being away on their honeymoon. Rebecca would perhaps be staying with some doddering old folks, relatives of the groom. She hadn't expected a man like Trey.

"*Trey* Waterson?" she confirmed. "Not Patricia's Luke?"

"James Waterson the third," Rebecca said quietly, taking pride in the name, although it really had nothing to do with her.

"You live here, then, James. And my daughter's been living with you. Sit down, and let's get to know one another better." She patted the table to indicate an empty chair.

Rebecca began to move toward it, but Trey stopped her by sliding his hand from her back to rest on her hip. Other than that, he didn't move at all.

She wished she were more like him; it hadn't occurred to Trey to obey her mother. She stood still, waiting for a scene to unfold that she hadn't foreseen. Never had she imagined that she'd face her mother with a man like Trey by her side.

Her mother tilted her head, studying Trey with her smile still in place. "You look like a cowboy, James. Do you not think you ought to meet with a girl's parent?"

Rebecca looked at Trey nervously. He didn't look nervous at all. He had that stoic cowboy look on his face, the one he wore most of the time, unless she teased a grin out of him.

It didn't sit well with her mother. "This isn't a suggestion. Where I come from, a man sits when he's invited to talk with a lady."

"You don't strike me as a person I'd like to sit down and talk with."

Her mother's gasp was loud enough to cover her own. Rebecca bit her lip. It was possible Trey hadn't meant to say that, but he looked very cool and unruffled. Her mother wasn't going to hear an *I didn't mean to say that*.

He'd meant it, and he said more. "If there is anything particular you'd like to say to me, Charlene, I suggest you say it now. You weren't invited into my home, and you'll be leaving it soon enough."

Rebecca held her breath.

Charlene stood and crossed her arms over her chest. "You want it that way? Fine. I'll make this simple for everyone to understand. You're shagging my daughter. You took her virginity. I don't see a ring on her finger."

Marriage. Of course, her mother would demand

marriage. Although Rebecca had broken the cardinal rule and Trey had gotten the milk for free, now her mother would demand that he buy the cow.

Tears stung her eyes. She didn't want a proposal wrung out of any man under duress. As she took a breath to beg her mother not to start with the marriage talk, Trey squeezed her hip, as if he wanted her to stay silent. Rebecca kept quiet and didn't beg.

Her mother kept talking. "Don't assume that I'm unhappy about that. Just the opposite. Thank God, there's no ring on her finger. She can do much better than a midcentury modern house in the middle of nowhere. But since you've felt free to enjoy her company, I want to know what you're going to do for her future. When you've had your fun, what is she going to have to show for it?"

"Mother, stop." It was so crass, Rebecca broke her silence. She felt her own blush.

"Do you think I'm going to keep that rental car on my credit card for one more day, Becky? Your boy here can pony up and buy you something decent to drive. You should have already arranged it, young lady."

"I don't want that." The discussion was making her feel cheap and tawdry, but worse, it was exposing every ugly truth about how she'd been raised. She'd told Trey about the stepfathers and the marriages, painting as positive a picture as she could of her life. With all these crass words, Trey's opinion of her had to fall. It was true she'd been raised with her mother's values. She'd never believed in them, but she felt guilty by association.

"You deserve a car, and more besides. Grow a spine, Becky Cargill. He took your virginity, for God's sake."

"Stop it." Rebecca stepped forward. "It's none of your business. I am none of your business."

"Hector was taking you to a seaside palace. He's got a rope of pearls in a velvet box ready for you, and that was just the first day's gift. There were to be treats every day. That's what I raised you for, to be treated like a princess. That's why I took you in, and made you a Cargill. I raised you with Maynards and Lexingtons. We've worked for this your whole life."

Rebecca whirled back toward Trey, who was still calm, studying her mother intently, taking in every word she said.

"Don't believe her," Rebecca said. "I don't want any of that. I never have."

Trey turned his gaze to her, studying her as he had her mother, as if he had all the time in the world. He placed his warm hand over hers; she hadn't realized she was clutching his sleeve. "You are the one I know, not her. I trust you. I'm just listening to the tale she's spinning. It's like watching a mare try to establish herself as boss of the corral. You watch her for a while to see if she's gonna calm down and fit in. If she doesn't, then you have to cut her from the herd. The rest of the horses don't want her around."

Rebecca wished her wobbly smile reflected her rock-solid heart better. She loved this man. She really did.

"I love your cowboy analogies."

He didn't grin, but he smoothed his fingertips over the back of her hand before moving away. "Some mares

never learn to get along. They get trailered and taken
to another ranch to become some other man's problem.
Charlene, it's time for you to go."

He gestured toward the living room, but Charlene
didn't move, so he took her by the arm and escorted
her with the proper cowboy manners she'd accused him
of lacking. Rebecca followed, so grateful the whole
dreaded encounter was ending that she forgot what
was waiting around the corner.

"Who the hell are you?" Trey demanded of the man
in his armchair. He released Charlene's arm with an
unceremonious push toward the front door and stood
with his hands loose by his sides.

Hector had come to his feet. His initial reaction was
a step back from Trey, but then he recollected himself
and stood his ground. Rebecca knew that was a mistake.

"Becky, I have no further time for your games."
Hector addressed her as if there weren't a six-foot-four
man in between them. "We're leaving, packed or not.
Get in the car with your mother."

Rebecca knew that was an even bigger mistake.

Trey crowded Hector's space, his words low, but the
language that reached Rebecca was far stronger than
anything she'd ever heard him use.

"Robert?" Hector called in a thin voice to the man
in the navy suit who'd been stationed by the door.

"You don't want to do that," Trey said, his gaze boring into Hector's as Robert came over at a jog.

It's like watching a train wreck. It was so obvious
what was going to happen. Rebecca couldn't turn away,

and so she saw Trey's smile the instant before he threw his shoulder into the doomed Robert's chest, knocking the man to the ground. Trey grabbed Hector by the throat. He twisted the collar of Hector's sweater in his fist. "One piece of advice. Do not tell me your name."

Rebecca could only assume Hector had been the boss of his own little world too long. He'd forgotten that power in a Boston bank office didn't mean he had any other kind of power. "I'm Hector Ferrique, and you better remember that name. I'm going to—"

Trey's fist was quick and efficient. Hector hit the ground with only one blow. Unfortunately, he took the table lamp down with him.

"Hector Ferrique, you owe my mother a lamp. Now get the hell off my land."

Chapter Seventeen

The rain began after Rebecca's mother left. Trey left Rebecca, too, to bring the horses in from the winter weather. He was gone a long time. There were a lot of horses, and two more barns farther from the house. The ranch was far larger than she'd first realized. Rebecca watched Trey disappear from her spot by the window.

She made a pantry dinner, boiling water for spaghetti and opening a jar of sauce, but she served it on china by the Christmas tree. She sat with her back to the winged armchair, and tried not to picture her mother's hand touching the mantel.

She felt Trey's gaze on her, and set aside her plate. "Not hungry?" he asked.

She looked up at him, prepared to shrug and smile and pretend. The care and concern in his summer blue eyes took her breath away. That was what she wanted most. That was what she'd failed to capture in her coupons.

The sex was important, though. It gave him a reason to keep her around, which kept her safe and provided for. She needed to lighten up this somber dinner. Keep it fun. Keep it sexy.

On the blanket by the tree, she drew her knees to her chest and clasped her arms around them, putting a little energy into her pose, tilting her head in a flirtatious way.

Trey was near her, sitting on the floor as well, but using the sofa as a backrest. He looked so wonderful, freshly showered, his black hair still damp. He was nearly done with an enormous portion of spaghetti. If she was going to play house with a man who worked outdoors all day, she was going to have to remember to cook for three. Maybe four.

She waited until he looked up from his plate, then she smiled as if she were perfectly delighted with life. "You were gone a long time. Did you miss me?"

"I keep you in my mind every minute."

"Oh." There was an intensity to his words that she wasn't prepared to hear. She'd been planning on steering the conversation in a different direction. "I guess there must be a lot of horses here, with all those different barns and paddocks. Is your ranch very big?"

"About seventy-five thousand acres."

"Seventy-five thousand?" The number boggled her mind and derailed her train of thought. "I never left the ranch when I ran away, did I?"

"You stayed right where I could find you."

Again, that intensity. Rebecca couldn't ignore it, so she relaxed enough to rest her chin on her knees. "You're the James in James Hill, I take it. Why didn't they call it Waterson Hill, or something like that?"

"The ranch is old. The only way to have one this size is to inherit it. Land costs too much to start a new cattle operation. Over time, the ranch got passed down through women every few generations. The last names would change. I'm the third James Waterson, but there were two James McClaines before that, and the original land grant was to James Schuler, my many-greats grandfather."

"You're the sixth James to own the James Hill Ranch. That's some old money." And then, to her mortification, she burst into tears. "My mother would be so proud of me."

He set his plate aside and moved closer to her. She shuddered when he sat a little behind her and wrapped his arms around her, because it made her feel like they were back in a sleeping bag. Fresh tears welled, but she tried not to cry too loudly. She wanted to hear every word as he called her *sweetheart* and *darlin'*.

Eventually, she mopped herself up with her dinner napkin. "It's just depressing that I turned out to be like her, after all."

"I don't see the resemblance."

"She has Hector. I have you. I keep telling myself you and I are different."

"We are."

"I had no idea who you were when I first slept with you. No idea at all. I want you to remember that."

"I'll remember." He started to do that wonderful, one-sided grin. "Although I'm not sure that's the most flattering sentiment. That doesn't make either one of us look very good."

"Don't make me laugh when I'm so miserable."

"My apologies."

She laid her head back on his familiar shoulder and turned her face into his neck. "I wanted to be with you when I thought you were a landscaper in Oklahoma. Remember that, too, okay? This was never a trap or a trick. I wasn't ever trying to cut a deal with a wealthy man."

"I really am a landscaper in Oklahoma. I've had a lot of time to think—"

A horrible thought occurred to her. She pushed away from him so she could turn around. "You're not just a landscaper, are you? You're probably some kind of landscaping tycoon."

His smile faltered. "I've got a few crews. Eight trucks. That's more than some, less than others."

"James Waterson the third, do you really? This is awful. My mother has to save face. You know she's looking you up on the internet right now, and she's probably cackling with glee that she'll have a good answer when she's asked about little Becky."

She sniffed again, not very sexy, and flexed her feet in her socks. She was too comfortable with him, when she should be a *femme fatale* to whom he was helplessly drawn like a moth to a flame.

"If I married you, she'd turn that into her personal triumph, like she'd auctioned off my virginity for seventy-five thousand acres."

The last of his smile died.

She tried to tease him like a fun girlfriend should. "What else have you done? Nothing will surprise me. Have you saved children from burning buildings? Invented a new gizmo? Won a major sporting event?"

He ran his fingers through her hair. "Your mother might read that I was the highest-ranked college quarterback in the nation at one point."

He said it like he was confessing that he'd once been a murderer. He was in such a strange mood.

"You're not kidding, are you?" Now it was her teasing smile that faltered as she remembered the day's drama. "The way you took that bodyguard out...that was like some kind of tackle, wasn't it? Then you threw that punch... I'm so sorry you had to fight for me."

"I'm not. It was my pleasure."

She picked up his right hand and kissed his knuckles. "Does it hurt? I didn't get a chance to ask you if you needed ice or anything before you left."

"Rebecca, I mean it when I say it was a pleasure. Maybe it's a guy thing, or a cowboy thing—hell, it's probably a caveman thing—but there's nothing more satisfying than knocking down some bastard who deserves it. When you first told me his name in that sleeping bag in the cabin, I knew his time was coming."

"Did you know who he was today, before he bragged about his name?"

His hand grasped hers. "I may be slow, but even I can put two and two together. Most of the time."

The card game. How could she have forgotten about that miserable card game?

She kissed his hand one more time, anxious to steer away from anything he didn't like. Her mother would never have brought up a subject that offended her protector, and Rebecca was grateful for Trey's protection. "Do you think Hector will come back?"

"No. That was his only play. He'll move on now. You're safe on this ranch, either way."

She wanted to crawl inside his skin, just to be totally safe. She huddled against his chest instead. "I think that bodyguard was here to ensure that I got in that car. If it had started raining sooner and you had gone off to the pastures..." Fear of what might have been made her shiver the same as the cold did.

Trey ran his hands down her arms, warming her.

She forced herself to say her fear out loud. "If you'd left to work the horses just a little bit sooner, I would've been dragged away. No policeman would've arrested a mother who was flying her daughter home on a private jet. Money lets men do a lot of things they shouldn't."

"Did you notice the ranch hands that were out front when I put Ferrique in the car? There were at least two. One on horseback, one walking over from the cattle sheds. Did you notice?"

"Kind of, now that you mention it. Did you press some kind of alarm?"

"There is a fire bell, but there was no need to use it. That limousine was out of place on the ranch. I couldn't see it from the barn, but the hands at the cattle shed could. They were coming to check it out. It's what you do on a ranch."

"Why?"

He shrugged. "It's always been that way. It probably goes back for centuries. You've got to know who is on your land, bad or good. Visitors get noticed. Those cowboys wouldn't have stood by if they saw a man forcing a woman into a car. You're safe on this ranch, sweetheart, even if I'm miles away. You can sleep well tonight."

The rain turned to ice. The sound of the drops pelting the window changed subtly to something sharper. Something less forgiving.

Trey lay on his back in the four-poster bed and cradled Rebecca to his chest. The sleet had blotted out all the starlight, but he could make out the contours of her shoulder and see her hand on the white pillow because of the faint glow from the tree lights she'd left on in the family room. They illuminated the open door of the suite in holiday colors, but Trey appreciated their light for a different reason. Every moment that his eyes were open, he liked to be able to see Rebecca. Commit her to memory. Never forget who he held, not for a millisecond.

He stopped stroking her hair and just held his hands still on her head for long minutes, keeping his own breathing carefully even. Her eyelashes blinked against his skin. She could not sleep.

"Does the sound of the storm bother you?" No matter how softly he spoke, his words seemed too brash in the darkness. "You could try wearing earplugs."

"Then I wouldn't be able to hear your heartbeat."

The sweetness was piercing. She should have been able to hear the impact of her words, so acutely did he feel it in the heart she was listening to.

"An acre of olive trees."

The escaped words hung in the air. Silently, he sent more after them, curse after curse.

"What does that mean?" she asked.

One more time, he gritted his teeth and apologized. "I didn't mean to say that."

"I know. Usually what you say is connected to the conversation, though. 'Rescue swimmer' took a little explanation, maybe, but it made sense. I don't understand olive trees."

"It's a long story."

He couldn't tell her. He couldn't ask her, not while she was torn up inside. She'd been essentially disowned by her mother today, who had shouted nasty last-minute things in the driveway as the bodyguard had tried to get his boss's mistress to sit in the car. Her contempt for Rebecca's choices had been poisonous. Nothing Trey could say would make it better.

I actually do want to marry you. That'll be seventy-five thousand acres—or a third of that, anyway. That's twenty-five thousand acres, a wedding ring, and I'll throw in a new car, because you need one. Pretty good deal for your virginity, wouldn't your mother say?

"Long stories are good." Rebecca slid off his chest to lay on her stomach next to him, propped up on her arms. "I can't sleep, anyway."

"It's a hard thing, to cut off ties with your family, even if you're better off without them."

"I wish I'd never met her."

It was an odd thing to say about a parent. He never thought in terms of meeting his parents.

"That makes me sound like an awful person," Rebecca whispered when he was silent. "It's not like she ever hit me or anything."

He rolled on his side to face her. "Do you remember meeting her? She said something today like 'that's why I took you in'? Is she not your birth mother?"

He could tell his question caused her pain. Her eyes were luminous in the almost-dark.

"Trey, my love, we already talked about that."

His heart was pierced again, not with sweetness, but with dread.

"In the kitchen, while I was waiting for the water to boil to make spaghetti, you asked me that same question."

He searched his mind. Nothing.

"We joked about how a watched pot never boils, so we could talk as long as we wanted while we stared at it. You asked me about that taking-me-in comment. She's not my birth mother."

Nothing. As far as he knew, this had never happened in his life.

"I told you my real name. I'm Rebecca Burgess, remember?"

Rebecca was not a Cargill. He'd drilled that into his head after a few mistakes. She'd never gone by Maynard or Lexington.

"Rebecca Burgess." He said it out loud, the name of the woman he loved, but he knew he'd forget it and have to be reminded.

There was one name she'd never use: Rebecca Waterson. Trey would never ask her to marry a man so unworthy of her.

He couldn't remember boiling a goddamned pot of spaghetti. Disgusted, angry, he rolled out of bed and yanked on the jeans he'd thrown over a chair.

"Where are you going?" The concern in Rebecca's voice was precariously close to pity.

"Nowhere. My life is going absolutely goddamned nowhere."

He slammed the bedroom door behind himself.

Out of habit, he forced out the usual words. "I didn't mean to say that."

There was no one around to hear.

Chapter Eighteen

Rebecca was scared out of her mind. She'd been scared of being forced to sleep with Hector Ferrique and scared that Patricia Cargill would kick her out. She was scared of ice storms and hospitals, and she was still scared she'd somehow freeze to death in this warm house. But nothing, nothing, scared her like the thought of losing Trey.

Her hands shook as she tied the sash of the white bathrobe. She fumbled with the doorknob, but she held up the long hem of her robe and did not trip as she ran after Trey. He was not by the Christmas tree, brooding into the cold hearth, and not in the kitchen, where they'd had a long talk he didn't remember. She opened the door to the room he'd been in the first night, the room full of trophies that gleamed in the dark.

He wasn't in the house at all.

"Trey!"

At a full run, her fists full of white robe, she plunged out the mudroom door and off the back deck into the icy sleet, heading for the barn. She would cut through that to reach the ATV shed. Maybe he'd needed to leave, just leave, to escape a bad situation that he couldn't change.

I'll go with you. I don't care.

She kept her head down against the sleet, but she was forced to run a little slower. The bare soles of her feet struck hard ground. Every piece of rock felt like a razor blade.

She heard the pounding of his running footsteps a second before he grabbed her around the waist and swung her into his arms, running the rest of the way to the barn. "Rebecca, damn it, what are you doing?"

It was dark but dry in the barn, cool enough that she could see the white puffs of their breaths as they stopped inside the door. Trey put her down and slid the door shut, then scowled as he looked her up and down. He cursed at her bare feet and scooped her up again to perch her on a stack of hay bales.

The hay pricked her thighs right through her thin robe. Trey grabbed a horse blanket and bent to dry her feet. His movements were brisk and the blanket was coarse as he chastised her. "Don't you ever do a thing like that again. You scared the hell out of me, running across the ranch like some kind of white ghost."

"You scared me first." She was wet and chilled, but inside she felt hot and angry and so incredibly relieved to have him in hand's reach, looking strong and healthy and furious.

Done with her feet, he stood and pitched the blanket into a corner. "I was standing on the front porch. Staying dry, like a normal person, when I heard my name. What the hell did you think you were doing?"

"I had to find you." She grabbed him by the only clothing he wore, grasping belt loops on his jeans and tugging him closer to stand between her knees. She twined her feet around the backs of his thighs as if that would keep him from running away.

She circled both arms around his neck to pull him close, but he resisted her for a second that lasted forever. When he gave in, his arms came around her and he held her too tightly against his chest. Crushed against him, she felt like she could breathe again.

"You thought I decided to walk to the barn in the sleet?" he muttered into her hair.

"I thought you went to get an ATV. Everyone goes crazy now and then. You're allowed to run away, but you have to take me with you. New rule. I have to take you with me, too."

"Rebecca."

"Do you want that? Please tell me you want that."

He was silent, although his hold on her didn't loosen.

It would have been so easy to slip into sex. With her robe open in front and his jeans easily unzipped, he could have been inside her with a single push. The physical reassurance would be a relief after the scare they'd given each other.

Instead, they stayed as they were, so close, not talking, not close enough. There was something terribly, terribly wrong. Whatever it was, he was not going to tell her.

It was harder than breaking out of her mother's prison, even harder than staying awake by an oak tree in the cold, but Rebecca had to know.

"Trey, what's wrong with you?"

Oh, he held her hard. His arms were incredibly strong, and emotion made his hold too tight. She did not try to get free.

"Why did you get a CT scan in the emergency room and I didn't?" At his continued silence, she asked the most frightening question of all. "Do you have a brain tumor?"

If you do, how am I going to live without you?

Hard on the heels of that selfish thought, she whispered, "You're not alone."

"It's not a brain tumor. It's not a stroke. I'm just... damaged."

He stopped crushing her with his arms, only to start touching her with his hands. He smoothed his palm over her cheek, his touch not entirely gentle, and buried his hand in her hair. He seemed to want to touch her everywhere at once, a desperate and emotional man. He grabbed a fistful of her bathrobe's lapel in one hand, holding it shut over her heart, but his other hand slipped inside to cup her breast.

"Don't you see?" he said over her lips, letting her go, touching her again, sliding his hands back in her hair and cupping her face. "I am alone. I've been alone for ten years." He kissed his way down her throat, pressing his hands into her back. "I want you. I want this, I want this so bad, but I don't get to keep it."

She tried to hold him steady as she smoothed his hair off his forehead. "You can keep me. You've got me."

"I forgot our conversation. God, I lost a moment

with you today. What if I forget you? There are people
I forget entirely."

Her heart broke for him as he took her mouth and
whispered her name. He kissed her again and again,
saying her name between each kiss.

"Trey," she said firmly, but he didn't hear her. The
muscles of his shoulders flexed as his hands roamed
over every part of her he could reach.

"Trey, can I help you remember?"

When he bent to kiss her, she put one hand on the
back of his head and pressed her forehead to his, wanting him to slow down. "If you forgot me, could I help
you remember? Is there anything I could do to help you
remember?"

The frantic pace slowed as he became more focused
on her. The sleet pelted the roof and a horse shifted in
her stall, but Rebecca still heard only silence when she
wanted to hear his voice.

She tried once more. "When you forget someone,
do you ever remember them again?"

"Sometimes, but only sometimes. In the helicopter, when Zach Bishop said his name, I remembered
him. Before that, I didn't know who the hell he was."

"Then I'll tell you that I'm Rebecca Burgess." She
kissed him on the cheek. "But you might remember
me as Rebecca Cargill." She kissed his other cheek.
"You can call me anything you like, as long as you
call me yours."

She wrapped her arms around him as tightly as she
could, and she held him as the shudders racked his
body, until he was cold and lonely no more.

* * *

Rebecca Burgess Cargill stood at the top of the ladder and reached to the top of the Christmas tree to take the angel down. She looked like an angel herself.

Trey was the selfish bastard who wanted to keep her.

She came halfway down the ladder and handed him the angel. "I'm going to get these high ornaments while I'm up here, okay?"

He'd stand here all day at the bottom of the ladder, holding it steady and keeping her safe. It seemed to be the one thing he could offer her with confidence. He could keep her safe. But the rest...

For ten years, he'd worried about himself. When the world got too noisy or busy or dizzying, he'd escaped to make himself more comfortable, leaving parties and stores and any other situation that challenged him. He hadn't thought about what the party's host or hostess felt. He hadn't cared that a store employee would find his half-full shopping cart and have to painstakingly put back everything. When Trey had blurted out impolite truths, he'd hated his own embarrassment. If he'd noticed that he'd caused someone else embarrassment, he'd only been angry because it increased his own tenfold.

He'd ended up building a life that fit him, and only him.

Rebecca came halfway down the ladder again to hand him a cluster of shiny baubles. "Sorry, there are a bunch of fragile ones in there." Back up the ladder she went.

His life was limited because it had to be. Where would that leave Rebecca?

Confined to a ranch because her husband felt disoriented everywhere else. Forced to attend parties without him, or to leave suddenly and early as they had at Christmas. Required to watch movies on a television set, because the big screen gave him headaches.

Jeez, he'd forgotten that last one. This morning, with her unique combination of deference and determination, Rebecca had gotten Trey to describe his problems. She'd noticed the numbers, the spontaneous comments and that he'd forgotten their conversation, of course. He'd added some difficulty putting faces with names. Finding a new address.

"I'm going to drop all of these if I even wiggle a finger. Let me just carry this bunch all the way down, so you can take them from me." She kissed him before she went back up the ladder.

He'd forgotten to mention the movie screen thing. He'd downplayed everything this morning. He thought his life was straightforward, but he'd made so many accommodations over the years, he didn't think about them anymore. He didn't know how different he was—but Rebecca would find out the hard way.

If he married her, he'd bring her down. As surely as she kept coming halfway down this ladder, she'd always be the one lowering herself to his damaged level. Potential was a terrible thing to lose. If she gave up hers voluntarily, it might haunt them both.

"Don't come down again. You're wearing yourself out with all these trips to hand me things."

She sat on the top step of the ladder. "How do you propose we undecorate the rest of this tree, then?"

"Drop them. I'll catch them."

"They'll break when they hit your hands."

"No, they won't. I have it on good authority that I've got soft hands."

She made a face at him like he was crazy. "I don't know who told you that, cowboy, but between the ranch and the landscaping, your hands are not soft. I love to have them on me, precisely because they aren't soft. My hands are soft."

"It's a football term. It means—you know, forget all that. Drop an ornament, and I'll catch it without breaking it."

It became a little game, once he caught the first few and she realized he didn't miss. She started dropping them in rapid succession, or dropping two at once. He caught them all, right-handed or left-handed, without moving far from the base of the ladder. Had it wobbled, he would have caught that first.

"You're like a juggler." As she stood to get more ornaments, she said, "Soft hands is a football term, huh? You know, I read an article once about football players. About a lot of different sports, actually, that could cause head trauma."

Trey knew what question was coming. "Yes, that was it."

"So, what are you doing about it?" She pulled an ornament off and dropped it without looking at him.

"Whoa." He caught it, anyway. "There's nothing to do about it. I forgot to tell you, movies are tough, and— Whoa. You might want to give me a heads-up before you drop things on me."

She sat on the top step again. "That's what the doctors say? There's nothing to do about it?"

"Doctors." He wished he could spit tobacco juice like Gus every time he said the word.

"Lana called about an hour ago, while you were at the paddock. She'd really like to see you this afternoon."

Nothing. He'd never heard the name *Lana* before.

"Did she now?" The generic reply usually bought him time. If the conversation carried on and he listened hard enough, he might figure out who was being talked about.

"Well, she wouldn't see you personally, of course."

He looked up at Rebecca with his face carefully neutral, and kept listening.

"Because the baby's only four weeks old."

And kept listening.

"Oh, Trey, I'm so sorry."

She knew. She saw right through him when he could fool other people.

"Lana is Braden MacDowell's wife, the one with the brand-new baby."

Rebecca waited, and Trey remembered. He nodded, once.

"Dr. Lana MacDowell is in charge of research at the hospital, and she called this morning because they're running a study you could be part of. It includes a memory clinic. It's some kind of rehab program where they try to strengthen memories."

He'd given up on getting better a long time ago. Rebecca's enthusiasm was youthful and probably naive, but it was also contagious.

"Your MacDowell friends have got some serious connections with that hospital, because they could get you in this afternoon for an evaluation. I have to turn in that rental car, so I thought we could go into Austin together and make a day of it."

Trey wanted Rebecca as intensely this morning as he had wanted her in the barn last night. There were no guarantees that he could keep her. His disability and her pity could tear them apart. As she sat so hopefully at the top of the ladder like an angel, he remembered when she'd looked as white as porcelain with pale blue lips. He'd been determined not to lose her then. He had to try to keep her now.

"This afternoon, then. We'll see what the doctors have to say."

Rebecca came flying down the ladder and nearly threw herself into his arms.

She was easy to catch. Trey was only afraid she'd be hard to hold on to.

Chapter Nineteen

The doctors loved Trey.

He did not love them.

Ten years ago, he'd learned to hate the word *unremarkable*. Every test had been unremarkable in its results. He'd been accused of taking drugs as an explanation for his symptoms.

Now, he was an *interesting* case.

Hours of testing had cataloged and quantified all his shortcomings. The rehab had started the next day. Even ten years after the damage had been done, the medical staff seemed confident that his brain could form new connections and improve its function—but modestly. The way they emphasized *modestly*, Trey didn't know whether to have hope or not.

The math and the disorientation and the rest were all issues that had their own specialists. This clinic focused on memory, and that was fine with Trey. The reason he was there was Rebecca. His one, overriding fear was that he would forget her.

Memory was a tricky thing, and in this, he was an interesting case, as well. Memories prior to his college days were still intact. The rhythms of the ranch, from the cycle of calving and culling to the seasonal demands of the weather, came easily to him because he'd learned it since birth.

The way he accessed those memories, like meeting Zach had opened all his high school football memories, made for an *interesting* case.

New information was harder to retain, like a new landscaping client's address—or a new person. He'd eventually remembered Aunt June, because she was an old memory. A new person, however, he could forget. Like Lana MacDowell.

Like Rebecca.

The key to putting new info into his memory, they said, included repetition. Had he met Rebecca at a party, he might have forgotten the next day that there was a woman he'd like to take out on a second date. But he'd met her in extreme circumstances, which made her more memorable, and they hadn't been apart since.

During their first day, they'd only been apart a few minutes, and they'd not only talked but touched. He'd learned the feel of her skin and the sound of her voice, without what they called environmental distractions, like phones or even other people passing them on a sidewalk.

If he and Rebecca hadn't liked one another, he would have stored the memory of an unpleasant person just as firmly.

Because sleep also impacted memory, the doctors told Trey that falling asleep with Rebecca every night and seeing her face every morning was exactly how they'd advise him to improve his memory of her, if it was needed.

They didn't think it was needed. His case was so very *interesting*. Given the unusual circumstances, they were certain she was in his memory now, just as the ranch and his parents and brother were. He'd never lost them, even if his brain hadn't transferred every conversation into long-term storage. He wouldn't lose Rebecca.

For that, Trey was grateful. If he returned to Oklahoma alone, he wanted to know exactly what his heart was missing.

For everything else, the doctors could go to hell. Their tests and their rehab were making everything worse, not better.

New Year's Eve was full of promise that the next year would be better, not worse.

Rebecca had looked forward to it every year for as long as she could remember. She'd hoped, year after year, that this would be the year she'd stay in one school. This would be the year her mother would let her choose her back-to-school outfit. This would be the year she'd meet a boy. It hadn't turned out that way, of course, but this was the year that would prove she'd been right to stay hopeful.

This was the year she'd begin a new life with Trey Waterson. He'd said so in the barn, five nights ago, on a rainy night full of raw emotion.

Kind of.

Every day since then, Trey had been at the hospital, throwing himself into rehab. It was all card games and puzzles, according to him, but Rebecca could see it made him tired in a way that ranch work did not. During their time together, he'd been too exhausted for much talking. During their time apart, Rebecca had started reliving those moments in the barn.

He'd said he wanted her. He'd also said he couldn't have her. When she'd said *call me yours*, he hadn't said anything at all.

She rubbed her arms against the chill as Trey drove them back to the ranch in his pickup truck.

"Thank you for taking me out." Her voice was husky after shouting over the music. The honky-tonk they'd just left had been a new experience in loudness. She'd never heard anything like it at her mother's clubs.

The bar was the closest one to the ranch, and it had seemed like everyone remembered Trey from ten years ago. He'd been shaking hands with men and been kissed on the cheek by women practically nonstop. He'd gestured toward her and shouted *Rebecca Burgess* to introduce her to every person. People had shouted their own names back at her. The band had played on.

In other words, it had been a nightmare. No fun for her, because she knew it must have been a misery for him. Still, he'd stayed, looking great in his black shirt, blue jeans and black boots, every cowgirl's dream. She'd had to insist that she was ready to leave before midnight.

She wondered what he'd been trying to prove. She was afraid she was about to find out.

Trey parked in front of the house and turned off the

engine. The dashboard clock gave them fifteen minutes before the new year was about to begin.

Trey spoke first. "We can get inside and put the television on for the official countdown."

"I'd rather stay in the truck, if it's okay with you. You're going to tell me something awful, and I'd like to get it over with."

It had just been a guess on her part, but his silence was an awful answer in itself.

She kept her chin up. "You're not the only one who can be blunt, you know."

He chuckled at that. "Fair enough, but you were blunt on purpose. There's a difference."

Rebecca waited. If he wanted to tell her why they couldn't be together, she wasn't going to help him out any further.

"Today was only a half day at the hospital, because of New Year's Eve."

She hadn't expected to hear that. She waited a little longer.

"I didn't make it home early, because I got lost. I drove for almost an hour, until I hit Sixth Street. The restaurants and bars were already getting full with the early-out work crowd. I recognized some of the buildings, and then I was able to get back to the ranch from there, because I'd done it so many times as a teenager."

"That was a clever solution."

"No, it was an accident. I got out of a jam this time, but I'm guaranteed to have that kind of thing happen again. I took you to the bar tonight because I thought you'd enjoy it, but also because I wanted to see how much I could handle. I haven't pushed myself out of my comfort zone in a long time. How did I do?"

"I don't think you recognized half of those people, but I don't think they realized it."

"I did all right, then. That's good, because I got bad news at the clinic today."

She couldn't stay cool at that announcement and turned toward him anxiously. "Like what?"

He picked up her hand and kissed the back of it. "I'm fine, first of all. Please don't go all pale on me like that. They thought it was good news at the hospital. I've been doing this intensive training, and after eighteen total hours of work, they told me my test score had improved."

"How is that not good news?"

"Out of a possible ten points, my score went from five to five-point-three. That was it. Three-tenths of a point. They call that a victory, but it was a reality check for me. There won't be any big leaps at this stage of the game."

"And because you're damaged, you don't want to marry me, do you? That's what you said in the barn. I just didn't want to hear it."

"Rebecca." Trey put his head back on the seat and rubbed his chest, as if she'd caused him some pain there. "That was prize-winningly blunt."

"*Damaged* was your word. I would never describe you as damaged. It's the last thing I think of around you."

"All right, let's cut to the chase. I want the best for you. If you were married to me, don't you see how it would be? You'd see a new place to eat in Austin. You'd call and say, 'Honey, meet me after work.' There's a good chance I wouldn't be able to find it. I'd be lost in town. You might have to leave your friends and come to find me. What kind of husband can't meet his wife after work?"

This was it, then. He was telling her that she would always have to deal with his brain injury. It wasn't going to improve dramatically, and he thought that made him a bad husband. She chose her words with care.

"You're asking the wrong question. My question is, why do you think I'd be such a terrible wife? Why would I ask you to find a new place you'd never been to before? Instead of telling you to meet me at a restaurant, I'd say, 'Tell one of the hands to feed the horses tonight. I'll be home soon, and I want you to go with me to a great new place everyone at work is raving about.'"

He was quiet for a long moment.

"Trey?"

"You can do so much better than me."

Her mother's words. She started to protest, but he cut her off.

"You can do so much better, but that doesn't mean I'm going to let you. What I was trying to say in the barn was that you are imprinted in my heart and on my soul. I was afraid my mind would forget you. It would be agony, because my heart and soul would know you were missing. At the clinic today, they told me what I already knew. You're already a part of me, like this land. That's not ever going to change. It's almost midnight. Can I take you for a little drive?"

Don't you want to kiss me? Don't you want to tell me you love me? How about ask me to marry you?

"Sure, we can go for a drive," she said.

He backed out of the driveway and took the dirt roads that went past the paddocks and the shed where the ATVs were kept. When he stopped the truck, he pulled the Navajo blanket out from behind the seat.

"First of all, happy new year."

Rebecca looked at the dashboard clock. "Oh, we missed it."

"No, we didn't. We've got the whole year. This is only day one, sweetheart. Promise one on day one is that I will never let you get cold. Will you come do some stargazing with me? There's something I have to show you."

Wrapped in Trey's arms inside the familiar warmth of the Navajo blanket, Rebecca sat on a little patch of land on the James Hill Ranch and waited. Anticipated. Savored the feeling of good things about to happen in her life.

She leaned back against Trey as he pointed in the dark. "Do you see that hill over there? It looks plain tonight, but this is its year. Let me tell you what I see when I look at that hill. I see potential."

Nestled into her lover's arms, Rebecca smiled as she listened. She was kissed, she was told she was loved and she was asked to become his bride.

This was the year that would start a lifetime of happiness. Throughout that long life, whenever her husband walked up behind her and whispered *an acre of olive trees*, she would know that what he was really saying was *I love you*.

Epilogue

The first year of the rest of their lives flew by. Trey sold his landscaping business and returned to run the ranch with his brother. Rebecca earned her first paycheck with Texas Rescue as an administrative assistant to her former stepsister and future sister-in-law. As winter arrived, the main house of the James Hill Ranch saw wedding preparations once again.

The new house on the hill that wasn't too far away was nearly built. The olive trees surrounding it were putting down their roots. And inside, Trey Waterson was bracing himself for a honeymoon trip.

He'd continued to make progress in his memory. He would never have the same abilities he'd had when he was nineteen, but someday he'd be able to quiz his kids on their multiplication tables. Someday.

First, he had to marry his bride, and then he had to take her on a honeymoon. It was no secret that he was more comfortable on the ranch than anywhere else in the world, but he and Rebecca made a good team and worked around his limitations, so Mr. and Mrs. Waterson were going to take a honeymoon trip…somewhere. Rebecca had planned it. Today was the big reveal.

He took a seat on the floor in front of the fireplace they hadn't used yet. Its first use was going to be as an easel, apparently.

"This is an artist's rendering, namely Patricia's. She's really good at interior design. Without further ado, may I reveal the Waterson honeymoon retreat? Ta-da!"

She set the sketchbook on the limestone hearth and sat next to Trey, scooting close. "It's our cabin. I want you to know that I spent a good portion of the budget having the walls rechinked. No cold air is going to come inside. There will be no need to borrow the blanket for certain necessities—ahem—because they make these cute little prefab cabin bathrooms that have water tanks and heaters. That was the first thing I had shipped in. The porch has been repaired, and there will be a giant pile of wood already chopped and dried and ready to go."

"You want to stay on the ranch?" He would be so much more comfortable here. That she was willing to sacrifice a trip to anywhere in the world for his sake made his chest hurt—nothing new when it came to Rebecca.

"Don't get all sappy on me. This is going to be a real honeymoon, where the couple get in bed and stay in bed." She looked at the sketch, and sighed as only a girl looking at a flower fantasy could. "The bed in question will have the world's most plush mattress. We could only fit a double, but that's okay because I always sleep on top of you, anyway, and it's a lot bigger than a sleeping bag, no matter what. There will be a down comforter and pillows. Wouldn't pillows have been so great last time?

"Everything is going to be white. All the bedding, all the flowers. And yes, there's going to be a garland over the fireplace that looks as pretty as a wedding gown, just like Patricia drew. She knows the florist who can do it.

"Best of all, we'll have baskets of food, easy stuff like wine and cheese, and champagne and strawberries. There will be a little propane stove in this corner, though, so we can make coffee. We can live on coffee and chocolate croissants. I've ordered an entire cheesecake, too."

He tried not to be sappy, and put a little fake disgruntlement into his voice. "For a sexual fantasy, you seem to have put an awful lot of thought into eating."

"I don't want to be cold or hungry. I'm taking care of the hungry part. You're taking care of the cold."

"How am I doing that?"

"Oh, I've got a whole book of coupons you're just going to love."

When James Waterson III married Rebecca Burgess and carried her over the threshold of their honeymoon cabin, he fed her a chocolate croissant, read the first coupon and they both started living happily ever after.

* * * * *

MILLS & BOON®

Why not subscribe?

Never miss a title and save money too!

Here's what's available to you if you join the exclusive **Mills & Boon Book Club** today:

✦ *Titles up to a month ahead of the shops*
✦ *Amazing discounts*
✦ *Free P&P*
✦ *Earn Bonus Book points that can be redeemed against other titles and gifts*
✦ *Choose from monthly or pre-paid plans*

Still want more?

Well, if you join today we'll even give you
50% OFF your first parcel!

So visit **www.millsandboon.co.uk/subs**
or call Customer Relations on 020 8288 2888
to be a part of this exclusive Book Club!